T0307897

PRESSING FREEDOM

An investigative reporter for a statewide newspaper connects the dots on an interstate jewel fencing scheme which leads to the capital city mayor's door and implicates a would-be governor. The reporter, a Vietnam vet who keeps his black ops background under wraps, is attacked by rogue cops, who also threaten his daughter and his girlfriend. His USMC training, unknown to his assailants, saves him from serious injury, but danger on the national scene draws his attention. With a former United States Senator who shares his concern for the unstable new administration in Washington, the reporter finds himself in the midst of a plot to return the federal government to stability, but by means that shock him to the core. A political thriller born of our current national turmoil, this first novel by a seasoned journalist will leave the reader with wide eyes and a quickened heartbeat.

PRESSING FREEDOM

A Novel

ROGER ARMBRUST

Parkhurst Brothers Publishers
MARION, MICHIGAN

www.parkhurstbrothers.com

Parkhurst Brothers books are distributed to the trade through the Chicago Distribution Center, and may be ordered through Ingram Book Company, Baker & Taylor, Follett Library Resources and other book industry wholesalers. To order from Chicago Distribution Center, phone 1-800-621-2736 or send a fax to 800-621-8476. Copies of this and other Parkhurst Brothers Inc., Publishers titles are available to organizations and corporations for purchase in quantity by contacting Special Sales Department at our home office location, listed on our web site. Manuscript submission guidelines for this publishing company are available at our web site.

Printed in the United States of America

First Edition, 2017

2017 2018 2019 2020 2021 2022 16 15 14 13 12 11 10 9 8 7 6 5 4 3 2 1

Library of Congress Cataloging in Publication Data: [Pending]

ISBN: Hardback 978-1-62491-125-5

ISBN: e-book 978-1-62491-126-2

Parkhurst Brothers Publishers believes that the free and open exchange of ideas is essential for the maintenance of our freedoms. We support the First Amendment of the United States Constitution and encourage all citizens to study all sides of public policy questions, making up their own minds. Closed minds cost a society dearly.

Cover and interior design by Linda D. Parkhurst, Ph.D.

Proofread by Bill and Barbara Paddack

Acquired for Parkhurst Brothers Publishers and edited by: Ted Parkhurst

122017

CONTENTS

1

THE BLACK CHEVROLET

FRANKLIN STUDIED THE STEAMING MUG OF COFFEE, knowing it was a mistake. But he slurped it in, tongue scorched, throat branded, sacrificing to find an immediate fix—provide that nervous consciousness so he could focus on writing the news story.

Far River City Manager Todd McCloud surprised the Board of Directors last night, halting them before they closed their regular Thursday meeting, and proposing a city income tax. It is the first effort by any city leader to impose such a tax locally.

Mayor Storm Weber, expressing irritation with McCloud's action, told the Evening Ledger, "I don't favor taxes, period, much less a city income tax." Chamber of Commerce President Brad Potter offered a similar complaint ....

Franklin had been back with the *Ledger* three years

now. He knew from experience where the writing would go with this specific story, and where the tax issue would wind up politically. Local TV, radio stations, and the morning paper, *The Republic*, had already reported the general story. Bob Starling, *The Republic*'s savvy city reporter, had recorded a solid piece explaining McCloud's proposal and the tax's legal implications. But he had struggled with a tight deadline, and wasn't able to concentrate on responses from the board or public.

So that would be Franklin's angle: quotes from the mayor, the board, the business community, the liberal activists pushing for the tax. This carried forward City Editor Ray Perry's philosophy of providing "fresh news" for the paper's afternoon and evening readers statewide.

7:15 a.m. Franklin had forty-five minutes to finish the piece for the state deadline. He would. Then offer an expanded version, with more colorful detail, for the city edition's 11:00 a.m. close.

"Franklin! You got it?"

Perry was glaring at him from the center-stage city desk. His bright blue eyes always glared, partly because of deadline stress, partly because of his magnified eyeglasses. When Franklin watched Perry's swollen eyes, he thought of Harry Truman, how his distorted lenses would display an expression of shock or surprise. Deceiving in both cases, because Truman had been extremely well-read, thoughtful, and highly aware. And that, too, was Perry, the type of journalist who—if commanded to choose between sacrificing his wife or freedom of the press—would go alone into an office and write a thorough editorial about it before letting people know his decision.

"I got it! In your hands at 7:35!"

Perry studied him in silence, scratched his graying steel-wire goatee, and went back to editing copy on his computer.

By 9:00 a.m. Terry Lester, the new cub reporter, was dropping copies of the first edition on each writer's desk. As expected, Franklin's story held the top spot. The banner headline: *City Income Tax for Far River?*

Franklin read through the story for any typos or problems. He knew Perry would be doing that, too. He glanced over at the city desk. Perry's head and upper body were hidden behind the open newspaper as he finished up the lead story's inside jump. His legs were stretched out and crossed, body leaning back slightly. Franklin thought he looked like a steady, sleek schooner with a pin-striped white sail. The sail slowly lowered. Perry glared over at Franklin, gritted his teeth, and dipped a single nod, "yes."

That was the near height of compliment from Ray Perry: his Pulitzer. Only once had Franklin and his cohorts heard Perry call out a compliment to a reporter. That was to Macy Collins, two years ago when he broke a state scandal that would eventually lead to the governor resigning.

"Collins!" Perry had shouted to him. "You got 'im!"

From Perry, that was the Nobel.

Noon now. Perry was single-nodding "yes" again after reviewing the city edition's front page. Franklin was irritable, involuntarily grinding his teeth, product of a third mug of coffee with no breakfast.

"Hey. Lunch."

Will Hollis was standing beside his desk, his own involuntary nods of a nervous head keeping beat with some internal music blended with a few sneaks of puffing grass out an open bathroom window.

Franklin grinned. "Lunch. Yeah."

At The Blue Plate a block away, Franklin ordered the meatloaf special and iced tea from Agnes, the pouchy, amiable waitress.

"You wanna roll?" asked Agnes.

"I don't know," Franklin smiled. "Do you?"

Agnes slapped him playfully on the shoulder and walked away.

Franklin looked at Hollis, who sat slouched and huffing his near-silent, breathless wheeze of a laugh.

"What's going with you and Janie?" Franklin asked him. "She forgiven you for forgetting her birthday?"

Hollis's glazed gray eyes, peering out from his wire-rim-circle glasses, gazed off into nowhere, then came back.

"I bought her a cuckoo clock," Hollis wheeze-laughed.

"Excuse me; did you say a cuckoo clock?"

"Yeah. She loves fuckin' cuckoo clocks. But she never

had one because her dad always hated them."

"But she hasn't lived at home for, what, ten years?"

"Twelve. Her dad's been dead for ten. But she's always been haunted by this parental-curse psychology, you know? This phobia that her dad's spirit would haunt her, or something, if she ever got a cuckoo clock. So I busted that fuckin' myth to pieces. The day after her birthday … my amends, you know … I hand her this beautifully-wrapped package. She rips it open and stares in shock at the clock. And I say, 'Janie, you listen to me. You have always loved and wanted a clock like this. But you've had this crazy fear of your dad. Well, he's not here now. I'm here now. I'm here to love you and protect you. Forever.'"

Franklin forced back the creeping snort.

"And she bought that line?"

Hollis was wheeze-laughing completely now, and gasped out a nearly inaudible "Yeah."

Then they both were laughing.

"Is there a cuckoo-clock superstore somewhere?" Franklin cracked.

"Don't know about that," Hollis said. "A month ago, she and I were driving out on Old Farm Road. Ran across this shanty of a store with a fancy name—Classic Antiques. Janie wanted to buy a lamp for her aunt. She saw and drooled over a couple of cuckoos there. I remembered and went back. Got a pretty good price."

Agnes clanked down the lunch special, with roll.

Back at the paper, Franklin was contemplating a Sunday feature on Far River's hope to expand west and south by annexing large areas of the county.

Suddenly, Perry was yelling.

"Franklin, the cops called! They just stopped an alleged drug-store robbery! Allegedly killed the alleged robber. Allegedly at Main and Fourteenth. Get on over there." Perry's height of ironic humor was indulging "alleged." Especially with information from politicians or the police.

"Where's Salisbury? He's the cop reporter."

Now Perry really *was* glaring.

"He's there. Needs back up. I want you over there to get the facts, then get the city manager and board's responses since they've been bitching about the crime rate. Call me when you're done."

"How am I going to call you?"

"Franklin, when are you gonna get a smartphone?"

"When you pay me more," he cracked with a smile, moving away from Perry's muffled grumbling.

By the time Franklin arrived, the ambulance was hauling away the body. Only a police captain and a couple more blues remained. Bart Salisbury, plump, slumped like a nose guard with too many tackles, was interviewing the captain. Ken Pearson, the paper's near-mute, ever-award-winning photographer, was storing his camera in his old gray Buick.

"Got some gold medals in that camera today, Kenny?"

Franklin asked lightly.

Pearson smiled and nodded affirmatively, wordlessly slipping into his ghostly car, waving and peeling out, disturbing the two blues.

Franklin studied the area, then stood waiting for Salisbury to finish his interview. He did, saw Franklin and, struggling to unload and light a filtered cigarette, walked over to him, his face seemingly puzzled at his cohort's presence.

"I'm not horning in, Salsy. Perry shoved me over here. Wants me to get the details and then query the mayor and board for their views."

"Rants on the exploding crime rate, right?"

"If it'll get 'em a vote, yeah."

Salisbury puffed away, peeking cautiously around to see if anyone was listening, a trait of paranoia Franklin had noticed in reporters who covered police departments.

"Guy musta been fuckin' high," Salisbury said. "According to Captain Edwards, he walked into the pharmacy, pulled a revolver, got money, then dashed out the front door onto the street still showing the gun. A patrol car happened to be passing. The two officers saw him running out, clearly armed. They stop, jump out, order him to halt. He points the gun at them. And that's his last minute on earth."

"Have you talked to the pharmacist?"

"Naw. I'm gonna do that now."

"Can I listen in?"

"Sure. C'mon."

Back at the paper, Franklin sat at his phone, interviewing Jim Butler, a lawyer and city board member. Butler hummed on about the need for "a reasonable approach to attacking the crime rate." Franklin listened and took notes on his computer, silently amused at the image of a reasonable assault. A computer icon and obnoxious "plunk" notified him of a new email. It was Salisbury sending him a copy of his just-filed story on the hold-up and shooting. Off the phone, Franklin began reading it. Salisbury's stories always were solid—brisk, brief sentences heavy on specifics.

Halfway through the reading, his phone rang.

"Reeves Franklin."

A man's low voice sounded nervous, timid.

"I, uh, I'd like to talk to someone about the police shooting a guy at the Main Street pharmacy."

"You mean the incident this afternoon?"

"Yeah."

"Bart Salisbury, our police reporter, is handling that. But he's not here right now. Can I help you?"

"I just saw a report on TV." Silence.

"Yeah? And?"

"They said a patrol car was passing by and saw this guy run out with a gun. That he aimed it at the two officers, and they shot him."

"Yeah, Salisbury's story reports that. It's the information the police released."

Silence. Then:

"That's not right."

"What's not right?"

"What the police are saying. That's not what happened."

"How do you know?"

"I was at the Sweden Crème across the street, getting a shake. I noticed a black Chevy pull up on the side street by the pharmacy, but didn't think much about it."

"A black Chevy."

"Yeah."

"At the pharmacy. So?"

"Then, two guys got out of the car. They barricaded themselves against it, facing the pharmacy. They were dressed in military type gear, you know? Helmets, flak jackets, carrying automatic rifles. That really got my attention. Made me move over and put my car between me and all that. I was in the parking lot cater-corner from them, you know?"

Franklin's mind began to calculate the scene. He knew the police had a special undercover team; they traveled in black Chevys. No other Chevys he'd seen in Far River looked like those, with their dull finish indicating the car bodies were armored. He leaned forward and started quietly typing on his keyboard, his notes of the conversation lining up on his monitor.

"Yeah, I know where the Sweden Crème is. What time was this?"

"Aw … twelve-thirty maybe. It all happened pretty fast."

"Go on."

"This guy came running out of the pharmacy's side door. Right across from them. And they unloaded on him. Shot him down."

"Not a passing patrol car? But a black Chevy, parked, and two armed men in military-style gear waiting on him to come out?"

"Yeah. That's right."

"He came out the side door, not the front, like the police said?"

"Yeah."

Franklin's gut was starting to knot, combined aftermath of the early morning coffees morphing with meatloaf, and sudden gravity of a possible police assassination. Then that distant past image suddenly flashing before him: the eye peering through the beaded curtain. He pushed it away, forcing himself back to the interview.

"Did the guy have a gun?"

"I couldn't tell. Maybe."

"What do you mean, 'maybe?'"

"Well, it looked like he was holding something, now you ask. But he wasn't waving it or pointing it like you would a gun. I don't know what it was."

"Then what happened?"

"Then a patrol car suddenly pulled up. Two officers got

out and went over to the guy's body to look at it. The other guys didn't even speak to them. They just got in their car and drove off. Except …"

"Yeah?"

"Well, before they did, they stopped and looked around, as if to see if anybody was watching. One saw me and pointed at me. The other guy looked. Then they both got in their car and got out of there."

"One pointed at you?"

"Yeah. But they didn't do anything."

"Could you identify them?"

"Gosh … It would be hard. They both wore helmets and sunglasses. They looked alike."

"Did you get a number on the patrol car? Maybe a license plate on the Chevy?"

"Naw. Shit, I was pretty rattled. And after that one guy pointed at me, and they left, I got the hell out of there."

"Could I have your name?"

"Aw … man … I don't think so. If that was the police killing that guy, I don't want them coming after me. I just hope they didn't photograph me or anything."

"What if I met with you. Anonymously. Don't use your name?"

"Aw … man … naw. I can't do that. I called because that report I heard on TV wasn't close to what I saw. I thought somebody should know. Hey … you're not recording or tracing this, are you?"

Click.

Franklin reviewed his notes. Then he scrolled to the top of the page, wrote a brief summary, and clicked "Print." Rising and slipping the page from the printer, he checked the wood-frame River City clock on the far wall:

5:17

Salisbury, Hollis, and the staff faithful would have gathered at The Caboose by now, taking advantage of happy hour. Franklin folded the page, grabbed his ancient blue blazer, slipped the paper in its breast pocket, and pulled the coat on as he headed out the side door.

⁓

Aptly named, The Caboose squeezed a lacquered rectangular bar, a dozen cocktail tables, and a small bandstand into a multi-windowed corner of shops lining Kennesaw Boulevard in Historic Highridge. The calm, talented Basil Matthews turned the small piano's keys into relaxing jazz.

The *Ledger* crew crowded around two tables, their booze and conversations flowing consistently the same as they had for decades: Government is screwed up. Business is screwed up. Unions are screwed up. Education's screwed up. Society's screwed up. TV and radio news are screwed up. Thank god we've got newspapers to save civilization.

Franklin had shared in the monologs as a learn-the-ropes reporter in the late '70s, cut away for New York at decade's end, hung on to Greenwich Village and newsprint turning to Internet until 2014, then retired back to Far River where he had planned to sit on his butt and write sonnets while somebody else tried to stalk news.

But he found he couldn't stay away.

"You oughta be in a fishing boat," Perry had scowled with a smile as Franklin sat with him at the city desk. "You don't wanna tread through this crap anymore."

"I'm dyin' here," Franklin had mumbled back. "How about tossing me a few general assignments."

Perry did. Also calling Franklin in to cover for senior reporters when they took their two-week vacations. The two veterans had followed that staggered pattern for three years now.

Franklin and his seltzer-and-lime drink snuggled into a table between the chatty Salisbury and still-mute Pearson.

"You still off the sauce, I see," Salisbury chided softly. "How long now?"

"Quarter century," Franklin muttered with a forced grin.

"Whoa! That makes me feel old," the police reporter moaned.

"Salsy, we *are* old," Franklin replied flatly.

Pearson sniffed a laugh, but said nothing.

"Got a little surprise for you," Franklin told Salsy, pulling the folded paper from his pocket and placing it on the table.

Salsy unfolded it and read. He seemed to stop breathing for a second. Then cracked a gallows smile.

"You get me a Pulitzer here, Reeves?"

"Make of it what you will," Franklin grinned. "Make that cop shop hop."

"Reeves, my man! Reeeeeeves!"

Hollis was gazing with glassy eyes from across the table, his smile indicating his ascendancy to a distant galaxy.

~

7:45 pm.

Franklin's maroon Toyota carried him through The Hills into a tree-thick subdivision where he parked outside a church, then headed to its basement. The Grace Place held meetings day and night. Franklin still made at least five a week, remembering his top priority: Sobriety, with a higher power first. Humans second. Yet it was only through these humans that he had first connected with a higher power. And he constantly met with them to recall that fact, and to return the favor.

After the gathering, he sat over a Sloe-Eyed Cow barbeque with Luke Whitman, a quick-witted lawyer and old friend.

"What do you hear about the city's annexation effort?" Whitman queried. Franklin knew Luke always tossed out a question he wanted to answer himself.

"Just starting to look at it. What do you hear?"

"Lots of land tracts for development out there," he grinned. "Lots of land with anonymous owners who could really use city services to up the sale prices."

"You got some anonymous folks you can help me morph into front-page stories?"

"Awwww, Reeves. You know I gotta honor attorney-client privileges. I never wanna cause trouble."

"Naw. None of you former prosecutors ever want to cause a problem."

They both laughed softly.

"How's Betty?" Franklin asked.

"She's about to retire. Get outta that investment crap. Nearly sunk us in 2008. But, boy, she rallied. And I was lucky enough to win a couple of big cases against nursing home chains."

"I read about those. One in North Carolina. The other, where, Wisconsin?"

"Land of the cheese and beer."

"Which you didn't partake in."

"Well, the cheese was good."

"Anybody on the city board got a land track in the annexation area?"

"Maybe."

"Any city hall employees?"

"Maybe. Of course, I can say that much because I don't have any board members or employees for clients."

Franklin knew that's as far as Luke would take it. But it was enough to warm the blood.

"City editor wants me to drive through that fifty-five square-mile area and write a feature about the proposed annexation."

"Ray Perry is a wise man," Luke drawled.

~

10:45.

Lights on in the Hillwood townhouse. Cassie was still up, lying on the couch, reading *Pride and Prejudice* ... again. Her dark hair short and neatly trimmed, sprinkled with bits of gray, her slender body clothed in navy-blue sweats, she seemed a sleek panther at ease after a chase. A Chopin nocturne dreamed on the stereo.

She raised her upper body to let Franklin slip in next to her, then rested her head in his lap. They both remained silent for a while, her continuing to read, him beginning to breathe deeply, focusing on relaxing.

It was their usual routine on a Friday evening. Saturday evening, they would dine out together, maybe hit a movie, live event, or party. Sunday, he'd cook her breakfast, her favorite omelet with salmon and basil, croissants and an espresso. They'd watch the evening mysteries on PBS, then she'd drive back to her small, well-kept Highridge home. During the week, they slept apart, allowing space for her to write her third novel, him to work on poetry and privately deal with sponsees.

Franklin noticed her yellow pad and pencil on the coffee table. She had sprung an idea and jotted down notes. She'd later incorporate them into the novel, or file them away for a later story.

Finally her soft voice kissed the silence.

"How ya doin', babe?"

"I'm enthralled by your hands."

"Never seen withered stems before?"

They both laughed softly.

"You lie," Franklin drawled in a near whisper.

He reached in his shirt pocket, lifted out a square-folded page, opened it and handed it to her. She read, no sound but the starts and stops of her breathing. Even Chopin seemed to pay attention.

YOUR HANDS

I love to watch your hands gently folding
on your lap, unfolding and crossing, shield
like Ammannati's Venus enfolding
her vagina—wary, caring, to yield
only for fiery Vulcan. Love to touch
your hands, dorsal delicate as your face,
feel your vein lines flowing life-blood with such
passion. Love to kiss your hands, gently trace
palms' lifelines with my lips, wet tongue explore
graceful ocean of your pores, taste lotion
of your blessed secretions. What can mean more
than your hands' adagio, slow motion
of your fingers caressing my resting hands,
guiding them home to your enchanting lands?

~

She inhaled quickly, let out an easy sigh.

"You write this for one of those young cuties at the paper?"

"I think not."

Her head still in his lap, she lifted her hands to his chest. He held them both, kissing them softly. Then her upper body rose, her hands reaching, touching his face, bringing his lips to hers, her clear eyes flowing through him.

Chopin prayed.

2

GAZING AT ORION

At 3:00 a.m., Franklin suddenly woke, as he often would do, memory stabbing at his gut. But he was used to it after these years. He didn't startle or waken Cassie. She only stirred slightly as he slid his chest gently away from her resting head.

Donning slippers and a sweatshirt, he moved from the bedroom down the carpeted steps to the living room, through the dining area to the sliding back door, quietly opening it and the screen door, stepping onto the dark patio. He stood, silently gazing up at Orion. As usual, he was perspiring, these brief psychic journeys back still challenging his conscience, seeing again the Franklin never seen by his workmates, friends, or loved ones. By no one now.

He had grown up in Far River, attended Catholic schools, had been an all-state basketball player at Catholic

High, went on to play for the local university. Then, after college, he joined the army. His record showed four years of uneventful service, working in maneuver support, keeping records and assuring supplies were shipped from Fort Leonard Wood eventually to American troops in Vietnam.

But his formal military record was all a lie, a cover. The fort was also home to a special detachment of Marines, and within that a secret squad for undercover missions. Army officers at the fort were under confidential instruction to seek potential candidates for the clandestine squad. They found a rare one in Franklin. His intelligence test scores were excellent, his athletic discipline and ability exceptional, and through the most stressful actions of combat training he had proved fearless, a great surprise only to him, it seemed.

Out of the blue, he had been ordered to report to a small building in a security-concealed area of the fort. Entering the unmarked structure's only door, guarded by two huge Marines, he found himself in a small front room with a single desk, behind which a beefy Marine sergeant glared inscrutably.

"Been expecting you," was all the Marine said. He rose, went to the lone closed door behind him, knocked, opened it, went inside and closed it. Within a minute, he exited, joined by a Marine colonel with eyes of an eagle focused on prey. He brought Franklin into his sparse office, shutting the door.

Motioning Franklin to one of the two metal chairs

facing the heavy, metal desk, the colonel sat, staring long at his candidate. Franklin, suspicious and uncomfortable, forced himself to return the stare, concentrating on trying not to blink. He knew this was something special, but not what or why.

"Are you willing to die for your country?" the colonel asked abruptly.

Franklin studied him, wanting to be careful in his response. He knew this guy didn't want just a gung-ho recruit. He was seeking intelligence and discipline, and no doubt quick thinking and action. But he also wanted insight.

"I've taken an oath to defend the Constitution of the United States, against all enemies both foreign and domestic," Franklin replied flatly. "I understood when I took that oath … exactly when I took that oath … I was putting my life on the line."

"How did you feel about that?"

"It is what it is, Colonel. I learned from years on the basketball court how the human mind and body can respond in ways it never realized to unexpected situations, and to react in the best way possible to support the team. It was all about what was good for the team. That was our corps. We trained ourselves daily to react as one. To be faster, quicker, more physical, more graceful, and smarter than the opponent. I knew when I took the military oath, the attitude would be the same, but consequences could be the most serious I would ever face. That I might not come out alive."

"Can you kill someone … the enemy … without hesitation?"

"I've learned to do that here. I figure those are my records you have in front of you, so you know that."

"You've learned to simulate that here," the colonel retorted. He picked up one of the sheets of paper on his desk and, looking at it, stepped around and directly behind Franklin, out of his vision. But Franklin had already surveyed the wall back of the desk, focusing on a large map framed with glass cover. In the reflection, he could still see the Marine.

The colonel with cat-quick speed lunged toward Franklin, his arms forming a choke hold on the soldier. But Franklin had seen his first step toward him, had braced himself, taken a deep breath, so when the stranglehold cut off his air, he still had full lungs. He had also begun rising, balanced from his chair, and was moving forward with the attack, the colonel unable to set himself and pull Franklin back. Franklin's strength and quickness used the Marine's forward motion to keep carrying him forward, flipping him over his head, the colonel landing with his back banging on the desk, and Franklin thrusting an open palm—rather than a tight fist—on the throat, leaving the colonel limp, gasping for breath.

Franklin knew that, if this was a fight to the death, the Marine could be able to react and keep the fight going. But it wasn't, and he didn't. The colonel lay there stunned only briefly. Then there was silence. Then he began to laugh, pulled himself to his feet on the far side of the desk, and continued to stare at Franklin. Franklin was not laughing, his eyes focused on his assailant.

The colonel sat down, coughing to clear his throat, but smiling.

"As you were, soldier," the colonel said.

Franklin sat and watched him, the colonel studying his eyes, then his upper body to see its reaction. The young soldier's eyes were intense, but he was breathing easily.

"You could have killed me then, but didn't," the colonel observed.

"Yes sir."

"Why didn't you?"

"You're not the enemy, sir. You're a part of the team. This was only scrimmage. You have to understand exactly where you are and who you're dealing with."

"But if I was the enemy, you would have killed me?"

"If I had any doubt before I walked in here, sir, I don't have any doubt now. I definitely would have killed you. But it probably would have been for me, and not the team."

"Soldier, what we're going to ask you to do is kill for the team. In some cases, killing will be the last resort. But in some cases it will be the primary mission."

"I understand."

And he did understand. He proved that when he was quickly moved from his barracks, into secret training with the elite Marine squad. And once he had excelled in the training, he had moved out with the squad in the dead of night, and been flown overseas to apply intelligence research and cunning, and often to kill.

No one back home had ever been made aware of this. Not his family, not friends, not his former wife or daughter, not Cassie. He had been sworn to secrecy, especially to protect his fellow squad members, but also their highly classified military missions.

Once, when doing a Fifth Step with his sponsor—admitting to God, another person, and himself his list of wrongdoings—he spoke of this in the most general of ways, in order to maintain the required honesty for the Step—so that no secret might lead him to drink again—but to also assure the confidentiality.

"When I was in the military service," he had told his sponsor, "I was required to kill, and there were times when I had to." That's all he said, but it was honest, and he believed it was enough.

Still, sometimes the memories would leap up, clear as if happening again. Usually when that occurred, he would immediately move to a private place, praying until the regret had lifted.

A couple of times, for personal therapy, he had written sonnets about missions. After writing them in longhand, he had memorized the lines, then burned those pages.

That had occurred years ago, but he still remembered

the poems. And as he stood on his back patio this night, gazing at those distant stars, he recalled one, whispering it to himself:

FESTIVAL OF THE SPIRITS

My wife and I stand on Dahanyang Peak
able to spy a cove of Lake Poyang
where hundreds of citizens cast small teak
boats, each with a lighted candle, Jiujiang's
honoring the dead...I've never confessed
how twenty years ago, on an August
night like this, I crept—a killer, noiseless—
through a small lodge here, the general's lust
quelled when I slit his throat, his concubine's
windpipe crushed with one blow. The lovers shook
as though passion still danced.
I slipped through pines
for hours. Rendezvoused. The Cav chopper took
me back to Khe Sanh … *Candles glow like miles*
of stars, she says, gazing at me. I smile.

~

He flinched, suddenly brought back by Cassie's arms encircling, gently embracing him.

"It's February," she whispered, kissing him on the neck. "You want to catch pneumonia. So I'll have to take care of you. Right?"

He turned to her, covering her with his own warm embrace. After a quiet moment, he flexed, lifted her off her feet, and carried her inside as she giggled and they kissed.

~

Saturday. 7:30 a.m.

Franklin was halfway through his workout at Pump Station. His routine was the same three times a week. He'd begin by walking, then running five miles on the treadmill. Move to the stationary bike. Then to the free weights, concentrating on deep breathing, pinching his buttocks and stretching his spine to keep his upper body straight, even when bending to pick up or lower the weight. Then to the big bag for his hand-and-feet combat exercises. Then the jump rope. Then the shower.

As he punished the big bag, he thought of Fitzgerald, Fitz for short, in New York. He'd be performing the same workout, just as they'd been trained to use it decades earlier. All the elite squad were gone now except for these two. Even Franklin's old sponsor, who had heard his confidential confession of military killing, had died. Franklin had gathered with Fitzgerald secretly in New York when both were there in the '90s, but only rarely when they felt they needed to communicate to survive. Always making first contact through a secret code.

~

"You ever miss it?" Fitz had asked him at their last meeting.

They were seated at Pane e Cioccolato, in Greenwich Village's NYU area, dressed in the most drab of clothing to remain unnoticed. It was their only time in public together, when they finally felt they could sit quietly and have a meal, thirty years after their deadly days.

"No," Franklin murmured softly, looking straight into Fitz's eyes the color of County Kildare's Grand Canal.

"I don't believe you," Fitz snarled softly, his mouth hinting a smile as he sipped on a Black and Tan.

"No," Franklin repeated, nursing a peppermint tea. "I don't miss it. Do you ever miss it?"

"Yeah. At night it comes back real clear. Gets my blood boiling. Especially those stifling, humid summer nights. Remind me sometimes of 'Nam, sometimes the Middle East."

A Bronx native, Fitz had returned to New York after the military and stayed. Worked construction in all weather. But that was deceptive. A job which his body could handle with relative ease. A job which did not torture his psyche. Fitz's mind was like a merging of the Louvre and the Museum of Natural History. His vast memory could soak you with the entire history of the Irish people, their dynasties and geographical locations on the Emerald Isle, their migration and specific settlings in America.

He had learned to box when young, loved to fight, raw-knuckled and to the finish, meaning until the enemy couldn't get up. His handsome face had suffered its wounds, nature melding their scars as notches of character. His taut frame and square jaw would have made Michelangelo sing. And in the '90s it still made a number of maidens sing. But he wouldn't stay long. He couldn't and keep his history a secret. So he kept moving away from relationships, even changing his residence every year, easing to yet another of the metropolis's myriad historic streets.

After their dinner meeting, Fitz headed to a bar, Franklin to a meeting. That was in 2012. They agreed to never see each other or talk face-to-face again.

~

8:30 a.m.

Franklin entered the *Ledger*'s newsroom. He had no deadline to meet this day, but wanted to get a copy of the paper off the press.

"You not usually here on Saturday," Salisbury said, looking up from his keyboard.

"Couldn't stay away from you, Salsy," Franklin quipped. "Your shaving lotion's been haunting me."

"Don't wear shaving lotion."

"Then maybe it was that filthy gin you were quaffing last night at the Caboose."

Salsy huffed a laugh.

"Pleadin' guilty to that, Reeves, son."

Franklin looked over the front page, saw and read again Salsy's pharmacy-shooting story.

"What you gonna do about the info I gave you last night?" Franklin asked.

"Got a call in to the police chief. Hopin' for a Sunday front-pager."

"That will have some blues crapping and squirming."

“It *will* that. You’ll need to contact the mayor and board, too.”

“Not today, Salsy. That’ll be Monday. I’m off to meet a beautiful lady.”

“Monday’s cool. We can start milking this thing.”

~

Franklin joined Cassie at the Far River Arts Center for an exhibit of Ansel Adams’s early works. She was studying his black-and-white titled *Monolith: the Face of Half Dome, 1927.* The huge granite outcropping resembled a dark, mammoth, moist chopped tree trunk encircled by snow. But what held Franklin was the center of the monolith’s base: a cave-like indention, and peering from it a surreal form resembling an intense eye challenging the viewer.

Franklin’s mind flashed again to an eye glaring through a curtain, but he quickly blinked and breathed out to push it away.

“He climbed 4,000 feet through heavy snow to get this shot,” Cassie said. She was still gazing at the photo, not turning around, having heard Franklin’s quick rush of breath. “That brief pant of yours tells me you’re moved by this photo, too.”

“You see right through me without even looking,” Franklin quipped softly.

“That’s because I see you everywhere. Everywhere I look.”

He stepped beside her, placing his left arm gently

around her shoulders, she sliding her arm around his waist. Then they stood quietly, focusing with Adams.

They returned to their favorite lunch spot: Sicilian Pies in Highridge, an Esso station in the '60s, which closed and eventually turned into a two-story eatery. Joanie and Christian prepped fresh salads and Sicilian delight downstairs, took your orders, then sent you up a dozen gray and black-top steps to the warped-hexagon dining area, booths along the walls and six tables in the floor space. With windows on five of the six walls, it provided magical, slow-motion light filling and changing the room's hue as the day waltzed to night.

Today Cassie and Franklin decided on pasta, her with a Dr. Pepper, him a Diet Coke. She liked studying the room's light when they'd first arrive. And he liked studying her eyes, today mood-changing flashes like twin lighthouses, now delighting, then questioning, then pleading, then meditating, as if her entire history passed before her as she gazed.

Then she focused on him.

"The senator's having a party tonight," she said. "We're invited."

The senator was retired U.S. Sen. Carson Matthews. And his inviting Cassie was always a half-command, half-plea for help.

Cassie and Franklin had met as young reporters at the *Ledger* in the mid '70s. He used to love to watch her strut across the newsroom's black-and-white chessboard floor. He wrote one of his first published poems about her. It was in his free-verse days of brief lines and short poems, before he moved to more metered rhyme, and eventually to mostly sonnets.

CHECKMATE

looking down
at yourself
walking away
your slender legs
move long
over opposite squares
calculated rhythm
revealing the queen
impatient with the game

~

After a couple of years of solid work, she had caught Sen. Matthews's attention. He offered her a job as a press officer and later his communications director in his Washington office. By then, she was actually splitting time handling press in D.C., and both press and state politics in the senator's Far River beehive. She eventually married a Massachusetts senator's top aide, but it didn't take. She returned to Far River to have their baby girl, and settled in back home, working another year for the senator, then a four-year stint with the young governor, Dalton Fellows, who eventually would replace Matthews after he retired from Washington's upper chamber.

Franklin had known something about Cassie from his first year of working with her. She was smarter than he was;

smarter than the other reporters and editors; smarter than the senator and the governor and their crews of savvy politicos who were always maneuvering for position, but couldn't outmaneuver her caring for her bosses and, actually, for the state and country. Franklin had told her this more than once. But, as it goes with humans, she had trouble believing him. She could buffer that disbelief by turning the attention back on him.

"You're one of the most genuine humans I've ever known," she'd say to him.

He would smile and stay quiet. But he knew he tried to be genuine. It was required for sobriety, but also for honest journalism and, yes, the art of poetry. And he was genuine with her in his response to the party invite.

"I know you're not big on parties with politicians, but I'd like to go," she said.

"I'd like to go, too," Franklin returned.

"What?"

"It's the senator. I don't care for dealing with the current greedy bunch. But I do like sitting with him, hearing about Kennedy and Johnson, his view of Nixon's rise and fall, his special friendship with Wilbur Mills. His contrasting them to Reagan, Clinton and the vast difference in the two Bushes."

Cassie studied Franklin as his eyes looked past her, reviewing the phantom cavalcade of power. She waited on him to come back, and he did quickly.

"Mayor Weber will be there," she said. "You may want to prick him on the annexation proposal."

"You know I don't want to talk shop with you. I want to talk about you and me and art and culture and sports and the world water supply and, hell, even technology."

"Yeah. But I like talking shop with you. I kinda miss the ol' hoofing."

"Then get back into it."

"I said I miss it. I didn't say I need it."

"Except for novel material."

"Thou hast said it."

Their lunch lasted two hours, including half an hour to eat. That's what they loved about Sicilian Pies. Joanie and Christian let them linger at will. But if the two guests saw a crowd forming, they'd quickly give up their table to aid the eatery's profits.

They walked through Highridge's afternoon chill, window-shopping a little. Cassie would eventually run into someone she knew from all those political years. Her familiar face and voice were constantly catching a passerby's attention. Almost always she seemed to remember names and would introduce Franklin. If someone recognized her from several feet away, but she couldn't recall the name, she'd gently call out, "How are you?" That was Franklin's signal to move away casually and study another window, saving her any embarrassment of trying to introduce them. They had never talked about that. It just naturally happened once, setting the future stage.

~

A cold drizzle teased as they moved from Franklin's car to the senator's two-story, old-brick home in a quaint area of The Hills, where meandering streets surrounded Far River's original country club. The senator's wife, Georgia, stately and gracious as always, met them at the door, her greeting kind to Franklin, and deeply warm to Cassie—grateful recognition for the years the press genius had served her husband.

The couple stirred briefly together through the small crowds in the living and dining rooms, then broke away as Cassie stopped to speak to a former staffer. Franklin weaved his way toward the den, the senator's throne room. Two couples—a graying man with a brunette companion and a striking blonde on a thirty-something guy's arm—flanked Matthews as he waxed about the current political scene.

"They've got to get their act together about climate change," Matthews was saying, obviously speaking of both the White House and Congress. He noticed Franklin walking toward him, and smiled, adding, "But the neocons keep having their way, so it just might not happen. Reeves, agree or disagree?"

"I agree with that, if the neocons keep having their way," Reeves replied.

"What can stop the neocons, then?" the dark-haired woman asked.

"You." The senator was gazing directly into her eyes.

"Me?"

"You plural," Matthews said. "You the voters. And you'll need to get organized because you're fighting Big Money."

"You mean the military-industrial complex," the woman's male companion commented. "You've complained about them for years, Senator."

"Yeah, but now it's more complicated than that," Matthews responded.

"Now that we're an oligarchy rather than a democracy," Franklin heard himself saying.

The two couples looked at him in mixtures of confusion and shock. Matthews gave a slight smile.

"It has seemed to become the Wall Street-corporate media-military-industrial confusion," Matthews said. "Particularly with climate change. The Profit Cravers in finance and with corporations, particularly Big Oil, either deny or deviously combat climate change's reality. And the military is caught in the middle of that."

"You mean the military accepts climate change?" the lovely blonde asked.

Matthews turned to Franklin, not speaking but slightly raising his eyebrows, an invitation to move the conversation forward.

"The U.S. military has recognized climate change as a threat to national security—in fact, has tried to call it a threat to the nation—for over a decade," Franklin explained, making sure his eyes moved to each one in the group. "The armed forces' leadership has been seeking ways to go green, particularly in its massive fuel consumption. In fact, the White House … er … the former White House, issued a National Security Strategy paper. It raised climate change to a top-level risk along with terrorism, economic crises, and WMDs … weapons of mass destruction."

"But the new White House doesn't buy that," noted the thirty-something guy.

"That's right," Matthews said. "When the new administration took over, one of its first actions was to run that National Security Strategy through the paper shredder. And erase the term 'climate change' from the White House website."

"You make it sound like this could turn into a quagmire," the gray-haired man growled ominously.

Matthews said nothing, only giving a slight, matter-of-fact nod of assent.

~

As the evening wore on, Franklin found himself at the hors d'oeuvres table, munching on celery filled with an exotic cheese.

"Reeves, I wanted to say hello to you before we took off."

It was Mayor Weber, tall, paunchy, with a smile like a TV salesman for a vegetable slicer. His wife leaned against him, showing slight signs of having tipped too much. Both were wearing light raincoats, and he sported an eye-catching blue-grey fedora with the entire bill turned down.

"How are you Mayor? Mrs. Weber."

She smiled, glanced at him blankly, opening her mouth as if going to speak, but didn't.

"I don't want to talk about the proposed city income tax," Weber said with a slight laugh.

"I don't either," smiled Franklin. "Not tonight anyway. Man, that's a nice hat. Where can I get one like that?"

"In Kansash City," Weber's wife suddenly slurred. "He got it in Kansash City."

"No I didn't, Sylvia," Weber quickly countered.

"Yesh you did. Two weeksh ago when you flew to Kansash Ci …."

Weber had placed his arm around her waist, giving her a slight shake to hush her. Then pushed a forced smile toward Franklin.

"Guess we need to go," Weber said, moving them both toward the front door. "G'night."

"Good night," Franklin offered back.

"Sylvia likes the vodka." Cassie was standing beside him now, her hand placed gently on his left shoulder, watching the mayor and his wife exit.

"I know about that poison," Franklin responded softly. "The crowd's really thinned down. Guess we oughta go."

"The senator was asking for you," Cassie said. "He's

alone now in the den. Why don't you go and chat with him for a few. I'll see if I can assist Georgia in being kind to the hangers on."

Franklin found Matthews studying a column of shelved books.

"Picking out a bedtime volume?" Franklin asked.

"Let's sit down. I'm tired," Matthews said. He dropped into his favorite lounger. Franklin slid into the love seat a couple of feet away. The retired senator let out a long breath, gazing at the near, blazing fireplace. Franklin waited on him to start the conversation.

"How's Dalton doing from your perspective?"

"You should probably ask Cassie that," Franklin answered. "She used to work for him, and I'm sure is keeping up with him in the Senate. I've been more involved with the city and my own creative writing."

"Still writing sonnets?"

"I am."

"Good."

"I noticed Senator Fellows wasn't here tonight. In Washington, I guess, dealing with the new Congressional session."

"Yep. We're in trouble, Reeves."

"You mean the senator?"

"I mean the nation. It's a new age. We can't afford to treat Russia and China as foes anymore. World's too small."

"Climate change. We all breathe the same air."

"And we all disintegrate if a nuclear bomb explodes. Because one leads to many."

"I've written how we're in a new Cold War."

"We've never been out of the old one. But it seems, Reeves, my lad, we no longer have people in Washington who read history."

"Or have it read to them."

Matthews laughed out loud at that, then sat smiling sadly.

"What would Truman do?" Franklin asked.

"Not what he did in '45. After dropping those first two, they all knew they'd set a tragic precedent. Truman more than anybody, I believe. He was not only a prolific reader of history … I don't think he ever forgot anything he read."

~

Riding home, Franklin and Cassie relaxed, quietly listening to Beethoven on the satellite radio. Then:

"You and Carson didn't talk long."

"He was tired."

"And …"

"And concerned about civilization, basically. Climate change. Nuclear war. We didn't have any answers."

Back at his townhouse, Franklin opened the door for Cassie, followed her in, gave her a quick peck on the cheek and trotted upstairs. She knew what that meant, so she went into the kitchen, poured a small glass of her Chablis, turned on the local FM classical station, and sank into the living-room couch.

Mendelssohn's violin concerto was caught up in its early bravura.

Upstairs, Franklin turned left to his writing room, and sat at his computer fronting the two windows looking out over the parking lot and the Lutheran church across the street. He called up a blank Word document, and began by asking the Muse's guidance.

The words seemed to flow easily this night. They wrote quickly, he and the Muse, with only minor editing. Reading through the sonnet a couple of times, it simply felt finished. Still, he knew he could always return to it and make changes. Always, until it was published somewhere. Then, unlike Whitman, who immediately began editing *Leaves of Grass* when it came off the press, Franklin would leave the work to heaven. He thanked the Muse, printed out the sonnet, and headed downstairs.

By the time he sat on the couch next to Cassie, Mendelssohn had given way to Beethoven's moonlight.

She was half-awake, still seated, her head resting back. She turned her face to him, widening her eyes to help her become more alert.

"I started thinking about Christmas," Franklin nearly whispered.

"Last December? Our first Christmas together?"

"Yes."

He slipped her the typed sonnet.

Here or There

Sometimes I'm not sure where I am: here or
there. Here with you: Planet Earth, USA,
Far River. Or there: cosmic ether,
with everyone else, from Methuselah
to the not-yet born. Am I just sitting
in my cush chair, watching the NFL,
or floating in Neverland, forgetting
who I am or how my soul propelled
into this hazy state? I turn and see
you at the Christmas tree, your hands starting
to hang legions of lights. I rise, gently
take them from you, lift and spread their startling
glow along these highest branches. I look
at you smiling, watching me. I smile, too.

~

It seemed to Franklin that she would never stop reading it. Finally, she looked up at him, tears in her eyes. She leaned over and kissed him.

"Let's go to bed," she said.

And they did.

3

LET THE PEOPLE SPEAK

At the paper, Franklin wrote and filed a Monday morning follow-up to Salisbury's Sunday alleged police-assassination story, which included a quote from Police Chief Bill Wiggins saying he would investigate the allegations. Franklin noticed that Salsy had ended his article with a parenthetical sentence: "(*Reeves Franklin assisted on this story.*)"

The mayor and board members, of course, expressed shock at Salisbury's piece. The more conservative board members mumbled grave doubts about the single anonymous source; the more liberal directors called for an investigation. The county prosecutor vowed to uncover the truth.

Perry urged Franklin to move ahead with the Sunday annexation feature. So Franklin spent the afternoon driving south of Far River, weaving through the county's asphalt and dirt roads. He first looked for residents who might be sitting on a porch or working in a yard, querying them about coming into the city. The verdicts were fairly lopsided.

"They jes wanna tax us and run," drawled an elderly gentleman, rocking on his rickety porch, thumbs stretching his overalls' shoulder straps.

"They promisin' us police and fire protection?" a black woman, hoeing her garden, growled. "Kin ya see some white cop protectin' me?"

A Hispanic laborer, sitting on the back of his old pickup, laughed, "Senor, I move out here to stay away from city troubles. So you say now they bringin' them to me?"

The small businesses—mainly independent grocery stores, cafes, and garages—proved a bit more forgiving.

"If they'll fix the road so we can get more customers in here, that might be okay. But I've got my doubts," said Stagecoach Café's owner.

"You talkin' puttin' business taxes on us," complained Benny at his Benny's Garage. "They gonna havta convince me how I come out ahead on that."

"If they put a fire station and a police branch out here," then I might be for it," said the owner at Corner Grocery.

Eventually Franklin found himself driving down Old Farm Road, and suddenly spied the shanty Classic Antiques where Hollis had bought Janie's cuckoo clock. He decided to pull in for another interview.

A bell above the old door tinkled as he stepped inside.

A musty smell lingered as Franklin surveyed the stuffed shop that impersonated a hoarder's cramped home. Then, from a back room, appeared a gorgeous redhead. Early forties probably, Franklin thought. Stepping behind the cluttered counter, adjusting a couple of Tiffany lamps, she beamed at her new visitor.

"Hi! May I help you?"

Franklin's body flinched at her perfume when he was still five feet away. She wore a tight, short dark-blue dress, her chest decorated with a sparkling necklace.

"Hi. I'm Reeves Franklin with the *Ledger*. City Hall has proposed annexing this area. I'm traveling around, interviewing folks to see if they favor or oppose. How do you feel about it?"

"I'm Penny!" she perked, holding out her right hand, three of her fingers banded with glittering rings. "How do I feel about what? Being interviewed, or the annexation?"

She beamed more at her quip, and Franklin laughed easily.

"Both," he said.

"Gosh, you know, the county just raised property taxes. That hurt us. Now, if the city's gonna come out here and add more taxes …"

"This old building looks like it could use some strong fire protection," Franklin cut in.

Penny laughed and rolled her eyes.

"You noticed, huh? Yeah. I'll have to give you that. I

tell you what. They need to come out here and talk to us. Even visit our businesses and homes and see if we're really worth annexing."

"They're planning to have community meetings out here."

"Well … then we'll see how those go. Then we'll have a better idea."

Franklin could have thanked her then and left. But she was indeed attractive, so he looked to stay a little longer.

"I've a buddy who bought a cuckoo clock here."

"Yeah! We've got a couple more over there."

But Franklin's eyes stayed on her.

"Man, that necklace is lovely. Are those real diamonds?"

"As a matter of fact they are! But it's not mine. It's a part of our jewelry collection. And I love to model the goods!"

She held out both hands, each offering three shining rings. Then she quickly walked over to a glass counter, pointing at the jewelry inside. Franklin stepped over to take a look at the impressive display: necklaces, rings, bracelets, watches. He checked the prices, quickly seeing the items were quite valuable or else overpriced.

"That's an impressive haul," he remarked. "Where'd you get all that?"

"The boss loves to search out deals. He travels a lot. He has great taste, doesn't he? You want to buy something for your lady?" She glanced at him playfully, as if to question whether he had a lady.

"I may be back," Franklin grinned, moving toward the door. "Penny, thanks for the interview."

"Gosh, that was awfully brief!"

"You got more to say?"

"Yeah! Buy some jewelry!"

They both laughed as Franklin was leaving. Then he paused.

"Hey, Penny, what's your last name?"

"Shorter."

What's the owner's name?

"Perry Shorter."

"Oh … your husband?"

"No way! My big brother," she answered with a wink. "So c'mon back!"

Franklin chuckled, waved, and exited.

~

The late February sun was setting as Franklin stepped into the *Ledger* to type up his notes. He had spoken to twenty people, and felt he could use quotes from all of them. It would give a pretty broad view of county residents south of town, their honest attitudes clearly on display. In the next day or two, he'd head west of the city limits to gather more material.

The newsroom was deserted except for him and the night wire editor who sat at the room's other end. As Franklin was finishing his typing, Salsy hurried in, moved quickly to his desk and sat, looking shaken. He pulled out a cigarette, lit up, and began puffing breathlessly. Franklin rose and walked over to him.

"Salsy, Salsy. You know you can't smoke here."

Salsy glanced up, startled. He hadn't even seen Franklin.

"Oh … m-m-man … I'm g-g-glad you're here," Salsy stuttered between fast puffs.

"What's going on?"

"I had stopped off at the Clearwater Tavern for a quick one before going home. When I went back out to my car, two guys came out of nowhere and grabbed me. They shoved me up against the car, and one said, 'Get off the police shooting. You might get hurt.' Then they were gone as quick as they came."

"The police shooting. Did they mean the assassination story?"

"Yeah. I'm sure of it. It's the first shooting this year."

"What did they look like?"

"Hard to tell. The sun was low. They were wearing sunglasses, black bandanas, and hoodies, so tough to see any individual features. White guys. Strong."

"Do you think they were cops?"

"I don't know. I've covered other cop shootings, and beatings. But they've never bothered me before. Complained some, sure, at what I wrote. But never tried to really intimidate or manhandle me."

"You gonna write something about it?"

"Hell, I don't know what I'd write. There weren't any witnesses."

"Tell you what, tomorrow talk to Perry about it. Let him decide what to do."

"Yeah. I guess so."

Franklin firmly patted Salsy on the shoulder.

"You all right? You want me to follow you to the Caboose? You can have a drink to help settle you, and we can talk some more?"

"Yeah. Fuck yeah. I'd like that."

At the Caboose, Salsy began to relax as he sipped on his second Budweiser.

"You know what I'm thinking?" he asked Franklin.

"Sure. I'm psychic."

"I'm thinking whoever that was that threatened me—cops or not—this has got to be more than just some lowlife robbing a pharmacy."

"I think your thinking is good thinking."

"I'm thinking the robber must have had some connection to the cops. Must have known something they don't want known. He told the wrong person he was going to pull the pharmacy job, and they saw it as a good time to waste him."

"I'm thinking, then, that you want to know what they don't want you to know."

"That's what I'm thinking, too."

"So … tomorrow …."

"So tomorrow I'll talk to Perry about the shakedown. And I'll tell him I want to take my thinking to the police chief."

"Okay. Yeah. See what Perry says, and take it from there."

"Yeah."

Franklin studied his cohort, who now seemed pretty settled.

"Salsy, I'm going to head out. You want me to follow you home?"

"Naw. I'm gonna have one more beer, then roll."

~

Early Tuesday was one of Franklin's two swim days. Treadmill, bike, weights, and big bag on Mondays, Wednesdays and Saturdays. Swimming at the Pump Station pool on Tuesdays and Thursdays.

He concentrated on the crawl and backstroke, not counting pool lengths. Just swimming smoothly until he felt too tired to go another length, then going one anyway, as fast as he could sprint.

Rising from the water, he sat on a near bench, grabbed his towel, and began to dry off.

"Man, you *do* work out. Somebody paying you to suffer?"

It was Bret, the head trainer who worked personal sessions with the Station's members. Shaved head, ripped from shoulders to calves, he could easily be stalked by Mr.

Clean's ad agency.

"Keeps me young," Franklin quipped with a smile.

"I've been watching you for a while now. You're damn dedicated. Reeves, can I ask you something personal?"

"I got nuttin' ta hide," Franklin barked in a poor Cagney mimic.

"How old are you?"

"Sixty-eight years. And seventy-five days."

"Sixty-eight, huh?"

"And seventy-five days. Don't cheat me."

"Well, they say these days that seventy is the new fifty."

"C'mon, Bret. Don't age me any faster than nature demands."

How long have you been working out?"

"I've never stopped since high school. Actually started training harder after playing small-college basketball."

"Well, then. I'd say for you that sixty-eight … and seventy-five days … is the new forty!"

"Whoa! Hold on, Bret, my man. Don't tell Social Security. They'll cancel my monthly payments."

Bret laughed, slapped Franklin on the thigh, and walked off.

~

Around 1:00 p.m., Franklin met Cassie for lunch at the Salad Palace where they scarfed in the healthies.

"How's the novel coming?" he asked early on. The rest of the lunch their conversation stayed pretty one-sided.

Cassie needed to talk.

"I'm feeling blocked," she mumbled. "It came all of a sudden."

"Where are you?"

And she began to tell him at length, more to straighten it out in her own head rather than inform him. Which, of course, is what they both wanted. By the time lunch was over, she was smiling gratefully, hugged him tightly, and he her. Then she headed back to the computer, and Franklin drove west beyond the city limits for more annexation interviews. He felt satisfied with the handful he garnered.

Driving back into town, he decided to drop by Tom Mavis's office. A good friend, Mavis—graying and slender, an avid runner—was probably the most brilliant human Franklin had ever known, including golden minds he'd admired during his decades in New York. A trained economist who then decided to become a professional architect, Mavis possessed the uncanny ability to analyze every issue for its basic structure and financial worth. But he was also a talented artist and reader of philosophy, allowing him to, as he often would say, "connect the dots and see the light."

Franklin knew Mavis loved sitting in his small basement office in Historic Highridge, talking with him, largely because Franklin would play the interviewer, allowing his good friend to wax effortlessly. But he also waxed purely and logically, following general statements with detailed data. Both men would also take turns playing the devil's advocate, throwing in a controversial, and even sometimes outlandish, premise to argue.

Often, if they met on a Friday afternoon as Mavis was winding up the week's work, Barton Winslow would join them. A paunchy, mid-seventies retired businessman with snow-white hair and a photographic memory, Winslow and Mavis had molded a close friendship through forty years. Now in his mid-'60s, Mavis would immediately begin to smile when Winslow entered, knowing that the three-way banter could cover anything in the universe.

But this was Tuesday, so Mavis and Franklin sat alone, exercising their brains and wit.

"Tom, didn't you and the historic district folks meet with the mayor last week?" Franklin asked.

"Yessir."

"How'd that go?"

"Well, the mayor came in, prepared to tell us his great plans for our historic district. But before he could finish a second sentence, we sat him down and told him what *we* not only had planned, but had already started implementing to make the area sustainable."

"I'll bet that pissed him off."

"Well," Mavis smiled, "it shocked him. But, you know, politicians are kinda like sponge dolls. You can squeeze them as hard as you want, even crush them into near spheres, but they'll always pop back up, ready for more."

"But he got the idea who was in control?"

"Oh, yeah. The over two hundred voters there made that clear."

"He talk about the annexation at all?"

"He tried to. But we forced him to sit and listen to us. We weren't going to let him … what did the governor sing in *The Best Little Whorehouse in Texas*?... 'do a little sidestep'."

Mavis was a prophet of sustainability. He had begun to implement the theory back in the '70s, even before Toffler's *The Third Wave* became a best seller. Franklin loved sitting and listening of his desire for civilization's continuance, and how to achieve that in an age of deep greed, climate change, endless war, and globalization versus populism.

"Tip O'Neill was right: all politics is local. And the local community is the heart of sustainability," Mavis began. And he would go on for a while, like a patient steamboat down the Mississippi, resolutely taking you where he wanted you to go.

"I've written a few columns recently about world water supply," Franklin threw in.

"Bingo!" Mavis perked, his face brightening.

"Research around the globe's showing growing droughts and lowering water tables."

"We're in trouble," Mavis said softly.

"That's what Senator Matthews said. He was speaking of climate change. And nuclear war."

"Double bingo."

They looked at each other in silence. Then Franklin

surmised, "We *are* in trouble. Aren't we?"

Mavis winced and shrugged his shoulders.

~

Leaving Mavis's office, Franklin stepped into the parking lot, breathing in the sunset evening's chilled air. He raised the collar on his black, waist-length jacket, cradling it against his short, graying beard. He lowered tight on his shaved head the wool Colorado University ball cap his daughter Evelyn had sent him for his birthday last summer. He thought of her teaching there, a few states away. He thought of Mavis and climate change and droughts and nuclear war. He had written columns about all those and other vital issues for *The Catatonic Progressive*, a gutsy website out of New York.

Stepping through the near-empty parking lot to his Toyota, he pulled out his key. Maybe for his next column he'd write …

What must have been a body block slammed him against his car, stunning him. Then he felt four strong arms pressing against him, and a low, raspy voice growling.

"Listen, you old fuck. Lay off the police shooting. It could cost you your life."

"What … police shooting?" Franklin mumbled, getting his breath back.

"Oh, you're a funny old man, aren't you?" a second voice, higher and angry, said.

He felt four hands grab and flip him around to face

them. Two men in hoodies, with black bandanas and sunglasses. By now the shorter man—to Franklin's right—had pulled a revolver. He pressed the barrel against Franklin's forehead, the man on the left pushing a hand into Franklin's chest while he began drawing his own gun. They both moved a foot back to look Franklin over, then slapped up and down his body, making sure he wasn't armed.

"We can kill your fuckin' ass," snapped the high voiced man as he moved down Franklin's body. "And we can kill your fuckin' girlfriend, too."

As the two men stopped frisking him, and were rising back up, they began lowering their guns just enough. The henchman on the left snarled, "And we know you got a daughter in Colora …."

That's all it took. Both of Franklin's arms shot out in unison, the cupped crescents between his thumbs and forefingers hacking their windpipes, enough to sharply stun but not kill them as his fists surely would. Both men gave the same "glul" choking sound, their knees buckling, their guns falling to the pavement, sunglasses hurtling away. That set them up for two rapid kicks to the groin, bending both of them over, beginning their involuntary vomiting. The thug on the right struggled to recover, so received the first kick to the side of his head, inviting him to plop to the cold asphalt. The second assailant was limp, still undecided whether to gasp or puke. But Franklin chose to bust his head anyway.

As the two men lay quivering, gasping for air, Franklin

stomped each on the stomach, then repeated kicks to their kidneys until it was clear that neither man wanted to consider rising again. Franklin picked up their revolvers and pocketed them. Then he searched their back pockets. Both obviously thought they'd have an easy evening. They each had their wallets on them, along with their leather scabbards containing their IDs and police badges. Franklin pulled out his pen flashlight and compared their police IDs to their driver licenses in their wallets.

He walked around to where their heads lay within three feet of each other, bent on his haunches, and spoke softly.

"Lieutenant Bradley. And Sergeant Turner. Here's what's gonna happen. Can you both hear me?"

Two weak grunts came forth.

"Bart Salisbury … You know Salsy?"

Two weak grunts.

"Salsy and I are going to write a story for the *Ledger* about you. About your efforts to intimidate the press. About your efforts to cover up a police premeditated murder. And we're gonna keep looking and find out your involvement in this. And anybody else who was involved. You understand?"

Two weak grunts.

"Oh, and another thing … off the record …."

Franklin rose, stepped between them, lifted his right foot, slamming it down into one man's stomach, then the other. Neither was strong enough to howl, though both wanted to. Then he returned to their heads and his haunches.

"As I was saying … off the record. If you approach my girl friend or my daughter … if I even get word you're talking about them … or even thinking about them … you're going to wish you were back here tonight … still breathing … still hearing another living human being. Do I make myself clear?"

Too weak and in pain to grunt. Only near breathless "uhs."

"You tell your people this: I'm putting the word out to my people. And I don't mean the press. So if anything happens to me, they'll know about this off-the-record conversation. Then you'll all have very bad days. Long before you can get to my girlfriend or daughter. Yes?"

No sounds.

Franklin grabbed their heads, cracking them together.

"Yes?"

Two gurgling "uhs."

Franklin stuffed their wallets into their hoodie pockets, securing their badges and IDs into his own jacket.

"I'm going to borrow your IDs and badges to photograph for our *Ledger* story. I'll return them. I'm leaving you your wallets and drivers licenses so you can drive home."

Franklin stood, looked around the dark parking lot until he found, on the side of the building, the security camera some twenty yards away. He reached down, flipped back and gripped tightly the two men's hoods, dragging them to just below the camera. He then grabbed their back collars, bent his knees, and lifted the men to their powerless feet, turning their bodies and pointing their faces up to the camera, his body and face hidden behind them. He held them there for some sixty seconds, making sure their features were clearly recorded. Then he dropped both men back to the ground. Getting into his Toyota, he drove to the *Ledger* to write his story, emailing a copy to Salsy to add whatever he liked.

But before he wrote the story, he made two phone calls.

First, he called Cassie.

"I need for you to do something."

"Name it," she said softly.

"I need for you to put together some clothes and head to Sally's up at the lake. Talk Jackie into going with you."

"Reeves … what are you talking about?"

"We've run into a little problem with the police. A couple of them have threatened Salsy and me. Even mentioned you and Evelyn. I think it will all be straightened out in a week. But tonight you need to get out of town, for safety sake."

"If you're not going, I'm not going."

"Cassie, this isn't a fucking novel. These are guys who already set up and committed one murder."

"Well, you know Jackie's not only my daughter. She's an attorney. Double hard-headed."

"Then you'll have to double-emphasize to her that it's

serious. And it's not forever. Call me if you need me to talk with her."

"Can you tell me more?"

"You'll read it in the *Ledger.*"

"Of course I will. Damn. Reporters."

Franklin hung up and phoned Evelyn.

"H'llo."

"Hello, my dear daughter."

"Hey, dad. It's good to hear your voice."

"Evelyn, Salsy at the *Ledger* and I have run into a problem with a couple of rogue cops. They allegedly murdered a guy, and we've been investigating. Both Salsy and I've been threatened. And they also threatened Cassie and you."

"No shit!?!"

"We're not sure who all's involved in this crap. Whether it's just a handful of cops, or if it might stretch farther. I made clear to them we're aware of their threats, and we're writing about it in a story for the paper. But I don't know if that will scare them off. So I'm calling to alert you. Don't talk to strangers. Pay attention when you're out and about. Lock your doors …"

"I got it, dad. You taught me that well."

"You and Kurt still together?"

"Well, yeah. Duh."

"Does he have a gun?"

"Yeah. For hunting. I don't like it. But he has it."

"Okay. Talk to him."

"Okay. How's Cassie?"

"I've asked her and Jackie to head out of town."

"Mmm … okay. I get it. Serious."

"Yep … How's teaching anthropology?"

"Historic."

He smiled.

"How's making art?"

"Got a show next month. You'll get an invitation in the mail. Thanks for calling, dad. I love you. Take care of yourself."

"I'm working on that, sweetheart. Love you too."

Finished with his calls and his story, Franklin rose from his desk and walked the fifty feet to the photo lab. There he found the ever-dedicated Ken Pearson at his computer, adjusting sizes of some fresh photos.

"Kenny, I need you to snap these for my story I've just filed."

Franklin placed the two police badges and picture IDs on the table beside Pearson. The photographer stared at them in silence, then looked at Franklin, sniffed out a soft laugh, and grabbed his camera.

~

Back in his townhouse, Franklin trotted upstairs to the bedroom's walk-in closet. He pushed through a line of boxes to a small duffel bag. Opening it, he pulled out a bulgy packet tightly wrapped in waterproof material. Unwrapping it, he stood for a moment, gazing at the Glock 19 pistol and holstered Marine Corps fighting knife. Then he took them both, along with two fifteen-round magazines, walked back into his bedroom, loading the gun and placing the two weapons on the small table next to his bed.

He stepped back into the closet to three stacked boxes, removed the top two, and opened the third. He lifted out a half dozen photo albums, placing them on the beige carpeting that ran through most of the upstairs and downstairs, except for the bathrooms and kitchen. Then he pulled out a rectangular, dark iron file box some six inches high and two feet in length. The front was lined with four small combination wheels. Franklin rolled each one to specific letters and numbers, each producing a click, allowing him to open the top. He pulled out a laptop computer and cord, walked back in and sat on his bed, connecting the cord to the laptop and plugging the other end into a wall socket.

Clicking on the computer, he began entering encrypted codes, diving deep past the world's Surface Internet, down, down into the Dark Internet's vast sub-ocean of anonymous websites. His codes led him to a single site, its identity a brief line of symbols like, but not, hieroglyphics. On its message board he quickly typed his communication:

"Viper: My daughter needs anonymous protection. Immediately. Boulder, CO. I may be over-reacting, but better safe than ... Check my news story online tomorrow evening for details from my end. Here's her photo, home address and university building address where she teaches ...."

Within seconds of sending his message, Franklin's computer beeped, offering a response:

"Taipan: I'll immediately contact Denver, forward this info. Should be back to you in moments."

Franklin leaned back on his queen-sized rustic-style bed, resting his head on his contour pillow. He began the Serenity Prayer, knowing it would relax him. Within moments, a beep. The message:

"Taipan: Black Mamba concurs. En route to Boulder now."

Franklin let out a deep breath of relief. Then typed his brief reply.

"Grateful. Semper. Bless."

He clicked off the laptop, closed it, returned it to its file box and the box to its place in the closet.

He didn't know Black Mamba, but it didn't matter. He knew Viper intimately, and trusted he'd contacted the right person: someone who would stay out of sight, observe all, and move with unequaled speed to protect his daughter if danger rose.

Franklin dressed for bed, prayed to what Dylan Thomas calls "the close and holy darkness," and then he slept.

4

"A LITTLE KARATE"

The next morning, Franklin called Mavis.

"Who operates the security cameras in your building's parking lot," Franklin asked.

"Why? What's up?"

"I'm writing a story."

"Well … the landlord has a security room down from me in the basement. They monitor the cameras from there."

"Who's the landlord and what's his number?"

Mavis gave it to him.

"Is his office there in the building?"

"Yeah. Third floor."

"I'll pay him a visit. Thanks, Tom."

"Sure. Let me know if I can do anything to help."

"Will do."

~

Franklin sat in the manager's office at Burbridge Property Management. He explained to young Tom Bell how two men had attacked him in the parking lot the night before. That he was writing a story for the *Ledger.* That he needed to see the security-camera digital recording and get a copy to show his editor. He didn't mention that the two assailants were cops.

"I don't know," Bell said.

"Well," Franklin countered, "I can put in the story that you were unwilling to cooperate at bringing these thugs to justice. You think that might make your tenants consider leaving if you don't want to protect them?"

Bell escorted him to the security room where they reviewed the tape. After they finished watching, Franklin turned to Bell, who was staring at him with his mouth agape. Then Bell hurriedly rose and made Franklin a DVD copy.

Walking into the *Ledger*'s newsroom, Franklin headed straight to Salsy's desk. The police reporter looked up, smiled, and nodded toward Ray Perry who was seated at his computer, focused on the screen. Assistant City Editor Stuart DiMaggio, Macy Collins, Will Hollis, and the cub reporter Terry Lester surrounded him, all gazing at the monitor. The cub noticed Franklin, quickly nudged Hollis, and within seconds, all were staring at Franklin.

"Reeves you want to come over here?" Perry invited forcefully.

Franklin walked to them.

"I'm reading here that not only were you and Salsy threatened by two cops on two different occasions … but that you somehow disarmed both of them last night. Is that accurate?"

"Yes," Franklin said.

"And just how in hell did you do that?" Perry snapped in a disbelieving tone.

"I've got a recording of it."

"And where did you get that?"

"Today from the building's manager. Their security camera."

Perry couldn't help himself. He sniffed a laugh and shook his head.

"Well, then. Why don't we look at this recording."

They filed into the conference room and Perry stuck the disk into the DVD player. The crew sat silently watching. Only the cub reporter uttered a soft "Holy shit …" when Franklin was kicking the two officers.

After the recording ended, only silence. Franklin decided to break it.

"I thought we could get a frame of their faces and put it next to their photos on their police IDs."

"And how are we going to get their police IDs?" Perry asked with slight puzzlement.

"I told them I was borrowing them and would return them. Kenny's taken photos of them."

Perry stared at him with a mixture of confusion and

suspicion.

"Reeves … how the hell did you do that?"

"Do what?"

"Fight off those two guys?"

"Well … they taught us some self-defense in the army. And in New York I learned a little karate."

"A little karate," Perry repeated in disbelief.

"And I work out a lot, trying to stay in top shape. Plus I think they believed I was just another decrepit old guy. Probably gave me the upper hand."

Perry continued to stare at him.

"I'm sure Kenny has filed those photos by now," Franklin said calmly.

Kenny *had* filed them. Perry finished editing the story with a double byline for Franklin and Salisbury. The story included a Salisbury-garnered quote from the police chief expressing his shock and saying he'd immediately investigate.

"Okay, I've filed it and it will run in the city edition this afternoon," Perry said. "Now I'm gonna memo the managing editor and publisher, recommending we file a formal complaint with the police. I'll let you know how that goes."

"I think I'll grab a large *Ledger* manila envelope, put the badges, IDs and guns in it, seal and address it to the PD press officer. Take it down and ask him to return them," Franklin said.

Perry stared at him with a grimace, then shrugged and said, "Okay. Sure. We've got photos."

~

Franklin entered the front door of the police department's expansive one-story, cream-brick building next to City Hall. Stepping to the counter, he introduced himself and asked to see Sgt. Cal Leftwich, the press officer. Soon Leftwich arrived. Franklin knew the city edition had yet to hit the stands.

"Can I help you?" Leftwich asked.

"I wanted to return a couple of police badges, IDs, and guns."

"I'm sorry … what?"

Franklin handed him the large manila envelope.

"They belong to the two officers who the police chief said he's going to investigate."

"What … what are you talking about?"

Evidently the chief hadn't shared with his press officer the current state of affairs, Franklin thought. Or else he's simply playing ignorant.

"You can read about it in this evening's *Ledger*," Franklin said. "Thanks for your time."

He turned and left the building.

The next morning, Franklin's voice mail at the *Ledger* was filled with messages from the local TV and radio news stations, the *Republic*'s Bob Starling, and a writer from the local Associated Press office. He returned none of the calls, but began writing his annexation feature story.

About an hour into his story, Ray Perry walked by his desk, paused, and said, "The publisher's filing a formal complaint with the police and the prosecuting attorney's office. You may be hearing from the prosecutor."

Franklin looked at him and nodded calmly.

"You all right?" Perry asked.

Franklin nodded again, then went back to typing.

As he was winding up his feature, Salsy entered the newsroom and trotted over to Franklin.

"Our assailants have skipped town," Salsy said, grinning that I-got–a-front-pager smile.

"Where did they go?" Franklin asked.

"Don't know for sure. Maybe out of state, to parts unknown. The police are trying to trace them. The chief vows to find them and get to the bottom of the pharmacy shooting."

"You think he means it?"

"He'd better. Could mean his job. I need to write this up."

Salsy quickly moved away to his desk.

Franklin's phone rang. He picked it up, prepared to tell anybody in the media, "I can't comment. My statement is in the published *Ledger* story."

"Reeves Franklin."

"I'm lonely," Cassie's soft voice intoned.

"Aren't you with Sally and Jackie?"

"Yeah … but I'm not with you."

"Well, you're about to be. I've finished my annexation feature, and Salsy has the police story under control. And Jose Rodriguez, the city hall reporter, is back at work tomorrow."

"I miss talking to you. When are you gonna get a smartphone?"

"Clark Kent doesn't use a smartphone. He's gonna hit the phone booth, then fly up to protect you."

"I'll be watching the skies."

~

Before heading out of town, Franklin met with his sober sponsor at Juanita's Coffee and Bake Shop, a comfortable, quiet space connected to, but closed off from, Juanita's Brazilian Café in Historic Highcrest. The two men sat at a small table in the shop's far corner where they could talk quietly, their conversation overseen by one of Juanita's original paintings—a Brazilian beach centered with intense sunset, and on its right the deep-crimson glazed face of a laughing Latin beauty.

"I'm wondering if I over-reacted," Franklin confided.

"I read your news article," his sponsor said. "It was pretty general about your reaction. Said only that both men had revolvers, but you were able to disarm them."

"Yeah. I wanted to concentrate on the police activity, ranging from the pharmacy shooting, to the manhandling of Salsy, to the attack on me. Their string of assaults, not my response."

"So what did these two guys do to you exactly?"

"They hit me from behind with a body block, knocking me against my car, then whipped me around to face them. One guy put his revolver to my head, the other pointed his gun at me."

"How could you even think of trying to fight two guys in that situation?"

"They stepped back. Became comfortable for a second with being in control. I might have let it play out. I knew they had left Salsy unharmed when they confronted him. They might have with me, too."

"Why didn't you 'let it play out'?"

"They didn't stop with just me. They threatened Cassie. Then they threatened to go after my daughter. Blood and love run deep. I suddenly felt I had to take control."

The sponsor leaned back in his simple cane-back chair, adjusting his burly body. Franklin watched him breathe in the cascading aroma of fresh-baked pastry, then sip on his cappuccino. Franklin took a swig of his peppermint tea.

"So they're pointing loaded guns at you. They threaten you, then your girlfriend, then Evelyn."

"Yeah."

"Then what did you do?"

"I popped each in the throat, stunning them. That began to turn things my way."

"So you disarmed them?"

"Yes."

"Two men who said they would kill you."

"Yes."

"But you didn't kill them."

"No."

"Could you have?"

"Yes."

"But you didn't."

"No."

"So … how is that over-reacting?"

Franklin breathed in deeply, then let out a long sigh.

"I might have kicked them more than I should have."

"From their photo in the paper, they looked in pretty bad shape."

"Yeah. They both probably have internal injuries. That concerns me now."

"It does?"

"It does now. It didn't then."

"Why not?"

"My action felt appropriate."

"Maybe your action *was* appropriate."

"Maybe … yeah … But now … now I'm afraid I might drink over it."

"You don't want to drink over it."

"I don't?"

"No."

"How do you know?"

"Because you're not sitting in a bar. You're sitting in a coffee shop with another sober guy, getting honest about what's going on with you."

Franklin stared at his sponsor, breathed a soft laugh, and nodded his head.

"You know the deal," his sponsor said. "We follow our principles. And you and I have talked about what I believe: We're here to be of honest, unconditional love and service to everybody. In this case, you could have killed two guys, but you didn't."

"So, what now?"

"You pray for them. You pray they find the errors of their ways. You pray they turn their lives around like we have, with the help of a higher power. You … pray … for … them. And for everybody involved."

The sponsor scratched his premature gray, curly hair and gave a brief smile. He was younger than Franklin, a decade and a half younger. But he'd been sober twenty years. And he worked the principles constantly. Franklin trusted him. He knew what worked. So did Franklin, but he often needed another sober person to remind him of the reality. He'd pray for them. And everybody involved.

Franklin gulped down his now-lukewarm beverage.

"Gotta hit the highway," he said, rising.

"Think I'll relax and finish my coffee," his friend said.

"Got something for you."

Franklin reached in his jacket's breast pocket, pulled

out a folded sheet of paper and set it on the table by his mentor's elbow. Whenever he'd written a poem about or mentioning drinking or sobriety, he'd make a copy and share it with him.

"Thanks," his sponsor said. "I'm glad you do this."

After Franklin had left, the man unfolded the page and read its lines.

MOON DANCE

Li Po would drink alone, talk and sing to
the moon, dance and marvel how his shadow
followed his lead to perfection. I who
don't drink anymore still mirror his show:
sit and stare instead of sip, speak aloud,
sharing my sonnets, hum a Broadway tune
or Dylan's *Sad-Eyed Lady*, rise like cloud
beneath our beaming disk, knowing it soon
will slip through black-laced tree clusters, fragments
of light still commanding dark night like bent
giant's chip-toothed smile. Then this sacrament
of space will break free, gleaming to portray
black-pearl silhouette of my body's sway.

5

DEMONS REMEMBERED

FRANKLIN'S TOYOTA WAS ROLLING NORTH on the interstate away from Far River. He figured he had another hour of light left, the sun just now easing past the legions of oaks and pines lining the far-stretching highway's two sides.

He flipped on the satellite radio's '70s channel. The Doobie Brothers' "What a Fool Believes" rocked the car. "He came from somewhere back in her long ago ...." The eye through the curtain flashed in front of him. He pushed it away.

Then, out of nowhere, he was suddenly sailing back to New York and Heather.

He had met her when he was seven years sober, was warmed immediately by her sunrise hair and clear-river eyes, her mixture of determined voice and quick laugh, and the pinpoint imagery in her poetry. They had shared an evening poetry-writing class at NYU, developed a close relationship with the teacher who became their creative anchor. And they fell deep into each other.

By day, Franklin was banging out news stories, features and columns at the *Greenwich Gazette*, a small, old, respected newspaper covering primarily New York. But the paper's editor Max Grimsley gave Franklin a wide berth, letting him range from politics to the arts, even subjects national or international in scope.

Heather had engulfed herself in literature and journalism at Brown, graduated with honors. Carried that to New York, where she had grown up in Brooklyn, then a clean-cut suburb in northern New Jersey. She worked as a self-help book editor with a small publisher, the *Mason Press*, in the Village. She had pushed the money-minded young owner to upscale the product. The ambitious editor tightly hugged and nurtured new young, intelligent writers who touted snappy styles and deep desires to be of service to others. And she quickly moved up to a senior editor position. Now she was splitting her time editing by day and caressing her own writing by night.

She was also caressing Franklin by night. And she had taken up the guitar. He loved watching her gentle hands sometimes struggling, sometimes dancing over the strings; hearing her soft soprano creating impromptu lyrics, which she would pause and write down when they felt right.

But they were also struggling with their secret demons,

Franklin's known to him, Heather's repressed to the point she couldn't call up the source. Gradually she would.

Franklin's military past, the vital part he had vowed to keep secret, would rise at times to haunt him. He would suddenly leave Heather and his or her apartment abruptly, needing to simply walk through the night streets, sometimes sweating profusely, always pausing and sitting at a nearby park bench, praying the pain would pass. Eventually it did.

He would return to Heather, but feel unable to share honestly with her, only attribute his actions generally to the horror all soldiers shared in Vietnam—the illness doctors decades later would call Post-Traumatic Stress Disorder or Traumatic Brain Injury.

Her own traumatic history had involved the loss of her mother. When she was seven years old, living in Brooklyn, on a sunny Tuesday morning, her mother had walked her to the neighborhood grade school, kissed her and left. When Heather emerged at the school day's end, her mother wasn't there to pick her up. As she waited on the school steps, her engineer father suddenly appeared.

He was intense, grabbing her hand, only abruptly saying, "C'mon, honey."

Back in their apartment, he was equally abrupt, and obviously in shock, though young Heather didn't know what it was called.

"You're momma's not coming back. She has died. I'm taking you to Aunt Catherine's in Manhattan for a while."

He wasn't the type of man who knew how to hug or comfort her at such a time. He only left her sitting there sad and confused while he stuffed some of her clothes in a suitcase. Then he took her to his Peugeot and silently drove her across the Brooklyn Bridge and into the eighties and his sister's townhouse. She stayed there for a week.

They were haunting days of silences and stirrings, her aunt not knowing really what to say to her, not sure herself what all had occurred. She would take Heather on afternoon walks, unable to answer the child's constant repetitions:

"What happened to my momma?"

"When is my daddy coming for me?"

"How long am I going to have to stay here?"

Eventually her father did come for her. But he never told her where her mother had been buried. Nor ever spoke of her mother. Within a year, he had married again.

The trauma left Heather deeply bewildered and broken-hearted, her unanswered questions eventually leading her to brooding silences. When at home, she sheltered herself in her bedroom, feeding her lonely psyche with study, ferociously reading Sylvia Plath and Jane Austen. She grew into a brilliant, hardworking teen. Then an A student in college. But the suppressed sadness brought headaches. Years later, some of her lone moments with Franklin turned inward to sessions of bitter muteness. He learned he couldn't lift her from them, and so would simply stay close and supportive when he could. But there were times he could not, falling into the pain of his own past.

Still, they shared moments of deep connection: love of literature; love of going to the Village cinema for its classic old Bette Davis films and documentaries on Bob Dylan and Woodstock; love of the Village's Italian and French restaurants; love of laughing, and quiet, caring evenings together.

Their demons often would interrupt their nights of passion, him seeing so clearly the glaring eye through the beaded curtain. He would have to push away from her, his body shaking and sweating. Some nights her deep loneliness would erupt, blocking their intimacy, leaving her crying uncontrollably while he embraced her, feeling powerless in offering relief.

Eventually she decided to see a therapist. Heather would return to Franklin exhausted, the deep mining of her psyche frequently leaving her speechless in his presence. It made Franklin more insecure than he realized, often plunging him deep within himself.

He continued to write poetry to her. He had from the beginning, offering verse of their relationship. She had introduced him to tankas, leading him to experiment:

Oh, I'll try not to
adore you, much like ignoring
the moon this soft
September night crushing walls
of dark clouds with rushing light.

~

He would write simple verse, sharing how she was there with him even when not there:

AT MY DESK

I suddenly see the motion
of your soft guitarist hands
massaging each other with lotion
I gave you at Christmas, and
herbal aroma surrounds me
like mist on some mystery isle
glistening with ghost dreams
of your kiss, your whisper, your smile.

~

Then one February night, while dining at the Thompson Street health-food restaurant, he looked up from his brown rice and veggies to see her staring at him.

"I'm going to have to stop seeing some of my friends," she said.

"What is it?" he responded. "Your work with your therapist?"

She nodded yes.

He didn't know her "friends" included him.

After dinner, back at his Sullivan Street studio, they watched an old episode of the poetry series *Voices and Visions*. She wanted to see the section on Sylvia Plath. Then, in the darkness with Mendelssohn, they worked too hard at making love.

"I need to go home," she said. "Feed the cat."

She turned on the light, re-clothing herself in her

cashmere sweater, pleated tan dress and leather boots, then her navy-blue wool jacket and dark-gold beret. He slipped into his jeans, sweatshirt, wool socks and running shoes, donned his leather jacket and navy-blue beret, and walked her down the four flights of steps to the courtyard with broken fountain, through the old iron gate to Sullivan Street, and hailed her a cab.

She got in.

He looked at her and said, "I love you, babe."

Her face twisted, her clear blue eyes painfully burning, as if asking, "Did you not hear a word I said to you tonight?"

He was confused, shut the door, and the taxi drove off.

Around 2:00 a.m., he suddenly awoke from sleep, reality consuming him.

"Fuck," he whispered. "She's not coming back."

And she didn't come back. Over the next month he would call. She would speak briefly on the phone, her voice empty and absent. It led him to write:

Grief as Blowfish

Empty bladder thin
at first, then huffs up, a globe,
spiny fins stabbing
my bare sole, puffing poison
till my dead weight sinks below.

~

Then this:

SINCE WE NO LONGER TALK

who do I tell
of these gaping jonquils
and tulips cupped
like praying hands
huddled beneath
cherry blossoms
exploding in air

And finally symbolizing his despair:

KALEIDOSCOPE

Finally sick of missing you
I rub my penis erect
double-fold thick rubber band
forcing it over head
pushing it down shaft
to base at tip of testes
and watch stretching flesh
swell to purple-red
while I feel for handle
of butcher knife
grasping it with right hand
grabbing head with left
and flashing serrate blade
sharp as shark's teeth
clean through in two whacks
throwing knife to dirt-rug floor
and lying back on futon
I turn toward burning desk light
lift severed shaft to right eye

and rotate it slow as spit
while I gaze through head-spout
and marvel at melting patterns:
vein-blue snowflakes melding
with piss-yellow moon slits
and come-cream beams
all swirling into blood-bright lava
searing swiftly to black

~

He wouldn't send her this. He remained sensitive to her psychic challenges, and didn't want to hurt her. He tried to let her go.

It took a while. Soon after her leaving, he began to write sonnets, partly because their poetry mentor wrote sonnets, partly because of her leaving. He found energy and relief in the challenge of the tight fourteen line, iambic pentameter rhyme scheme . For the next couple of years, he only mailed her poetry twice, each a sonnet for her birthday. She never responded.

~

The sun had set, so Franklin flicked on the Toyota's headlights as he headed off the county highway and up the dirt road leading to the lake house.

He was crying. He prayed for Heather. The last he had heard a few years ago, she was married and the mother of two. He prayed for them. He prayed for his daughter and her mother, and Cassie, for Jackie and Sally. He prayed for his sober sponsor. For the two AWOL, injured cops.

He pulled up and parked the Toyota in front of the lake house.

Exiting the car, he quickly checked the surroundings for anything suspicious, donning his dark jacket with its concealed-but-easy accesses to his loaded revolver and knife. The thick trees hung windless, the curved path to the lake empty, the now-freezing night absent of birds' and crickets' calls.

Inside, Cassie's arms encircled his neck, her body pressing his in an embrace he returned firmly yet gently.

"You're just in time for Sally's pasta," she breathed softly into his ear.

"Sally's pasta?" he responded loud enough for their approaching hostess. "She who shames the Sicilians." Sally smiled and gave him a peck on the cheek. Jackie trotted up and repeated the welcome.

After dinner, they adjourned to the glassed-in den with its view of the moonlight reflected on the lake below. By the lone light of the fireplace, they chatted easily through the still night. Surrounded by the three women, Franklin would turn toward each as she spoke, but he was also looking beyond each through the glass, outside into the backgrounds, alert for any movement or hint of sudden reflective light.

At bedtime, he told Cassie to give him fifteen minutes to walk outside, relax and meditate. When out, he quietly circled the house, pausing often, his experienced eyes and ears studying each area. Satisfied, he returned inside, and to her.

It was so comforting, her lying against him in the dark. The firm mattress and detergent-sweet-smelling sheets, not the brand he and Cassie used for their washes, but pleasant and welcome.

"I saw what you were doing," she said softly.

"What was I doing?" he deadpanned.

"You were taking care of us. Acting comfortable in the den, but looking at us then past us, constantly glancing outside. Taking care of us."

"Guilty."

"And when you went outside. Reconnoitering."

"Trying to find a phone booth."

She laughed slightly. Then sang oh so softly, echoing Celi Bee from the '70s "Superman man man, I love you Superman man …."

His mouth joined hers, and they flew through the clouds.

The weekend streamed with salient conversations covering everything from national-to-local politics to literature. Sally spoke of the nearby college's intense research efforts to guard the lake from pollution. Jackie clarioned her stalwart case for women's equality. Cassie critiqued LeCarre's *The Spy Who Came in from the Cold.*

"I saw the film with Richard Burton and Clair Bloom maybe twenty years ago on cable," she explained. "I didn't want to read the novel until I had forgotten the film. But I can't forget the film. That austere black and white. The tight dialogue. And, my god, Burton at his best. Those pained eyes, and that classic voice. And … of course … the novel's even better."

The foursome walked the lakeshore in the afternoons, praising the clear, cold air, the radiant sun, waving at boat riders they didn't even know. Moved from laughing at corny jokes to moments of quiet meditation, breathing in nature's peace.

By night, more laughter and honest talk.

At one point, Sally chirped, "Reeves, read us some poetry."

"Didn't bring any books," he begged off.

Suddenly Jackie reached in the canvas bag next to her, pulled out a small paperback volume of his work, and tossed it into his lap. He looked up at her, and couldn't help but smile at her impish grin.

"Read the one about Thoreau," she said. "At my bookmark."

Franklin turned to the poem, paused, inhaled then let out a deep breath, and offered it to them:

Thoreau

Holding still for Maxham's daguerreotype—
his eyes glazed as if reading a tax bill,
neckbeard a crescent thicket, curdled stipe
of his boutonniere cuddling left lapel—
he's gazing back perhaps at Walden Pond,

sun dazzling birch-lined shore; or studying
just-sharpened pencil, how he searched to bond
graphite and clay. He's 39, dying
sap-flow slow from two decades of TB.
Six years left, he'll write of autumn, forest
trees, wild apples; cross the Great Lakes, and plea
for John Brown. He'll smile when dubbed *anarchist*,
read from *Civil Disobedience*. Tell
his dear aunt of God, *We've never quarreled*.

~

Through it all, Franklin paid attention, both to his trio and their surroundings. By bedtime both nights, he whispered a prayer of gratitude for safe, sober days.

6

JUST A BUSINESSMAN

HIS LEAVING LOVED ONES ALWAYS BROUGHT LONELINESS. On the highway, heading back to Far River, the sadness seemed to cut deeper. The tenseness of the times, he thought. And his getting older, reminded of the reality that it all ends. Then he suddenly smiled softly, thinking of John Travolta in the film *Michael*, the beer-drinking, chain-smoking archangel gazing out at earth's beauty, sighing, "I'm gonna miss all this so much."

With no story working, Franklin simply stopped by the *Ledger* to pick up his paycheck. Then he remembered he hadn't read his Sunday annexation feature, having no paper at the lake cabin, only checking the news on the radio as he returned to Far River. He grabbed the Sunday edition and looked over his front-page effort.

"Hey, Reeves."

Jose Rodriguez was hailing him from his desk where Reeves had filled in during the city hall reporter's vacation.

"Hey, Jose. How was your time away?"

"Miami has no winter," the short, slender young man smiled. "Deee-lightful. Hey, you got a call from Mayor Weber. He wants to talk to you about your annexation story."

"I'll bet. He had to suffer through a piece not written by his communications director. Life's hell."

They both grinned, and Jose went back to writing. Reeves sat in the empty desk next to him and continued reading. After a few moments, a body stepped up next to him. He looked up to see Salsy, glowing with an intense stare and ravenous smile.

"Would you like to join me at my desk for a lukewarm cup of coffee?" Salsy offered.

"What I've been dreaming about all morning," Franklin quipped.

"I just grabbed two cups from the vending machine."

Franklin pulled up a chair next to Salsy's cluttered habitat.

"I got a source who's offered some clarity on the pharmacy shooting."

"Who?"

"He who shall remain nameless."

"Okay."

"The guy who held up the pharmacy … name Terrence Farrow. A small-time hood from Kansas City. Shakedowns.

A little fraud. A little blackmail. But nothing that would stick. Then, in the last year, he moved up. Got involved in stealing jewelry."

"Developed good taste."

"Yeah, right? Well, he seems to have partnered into a little underground railroad, fencing diamonds, gold and such in a quadrangle trade route: Memphis, St. Louis, KC, and Far River."

"Why here?"

"Evidently has a contact here who's involved. Don't know who or how. Not yet, anyway."

"Somebody with a jewelry store?"

"Don't know. But it seems ol' Terrence screwed up. Got arrested during a heist in KC. A good attorney got him out on big bail money. He was awaiting trial … then something strange happened."

Salsy paused, smiling at Franklin.

"So … are we going to commercial, or you gonna continue the tale?"

"Somebody flew up from Fall River, brought ol' Terry back. Word is the cops were secluding him in some private place away from headquarters."

"Our two cops, you think?"

"Gotta be. I know he was being guarded by two undercover guys. Haven't proved the names yet. He was extradited to face charges for an alleged burglary here. But they didn't hold him in jail. Someplace else."

"They flew up to KC?"

"Nope. Not them. Don't know who. Somebody in authority. But whoever it was, they must have been afraid ol' Terrence might rat on them. Maybe even bring down the whole underground transport operation."

"So they brought him over here. Then for some reason let him go? And he went and held up a pharmacy while they were following him?"

"Better. They set him up. Told him they were letting him go. Even pushed him out of a car a couple of blocks from the pharmacy. Told him it would be an easy hit. He could rob it for some bucks that would get him out of town. But you know what?"

"Tell me."

"They gave him a jammed gun. Couldn't shoot even if Annie Oakley was aiming it. So he robbed the pharmacy … then walked out into a firing squad."

The two men studied each other. Franklin winced, his journalist's logic suddenly seeming to connect blinking dots that, like a good metaphor, offered no logical connection yet made sense.

"When did they bring ol' Terry over from Kansas City?"

"A week before the shooting."

Franklin looked away to the far wall, considering options. Then he shook his head, muttering inaudibly to himself.

"What?" chirped a curious Salsy.

"My head says no, but my gut says maybe. Lemme get online and see where it goes."

He grabbed his cup of coffee, gave a toasting nod with it to Salsy, and went to the desk next to Rodriguez, sitting and igniting the computer.

"You talk with the mayor?" Jose asked.

"Later," Franklin mumbled, his focus on the screen. "This now."

Rodriguez studied him for a few seconds, then returned to writing.

Franklin googled the state's secretary of state's website. When it flashed up, he clicked on "Corporate Filings." He thought a moment, then grabbed the newspaper with his annexation feature. Scanning through it, he came to his brief interview with Penny Shorter at Classic Antiques, focusing on the line, "She manages the antique store owned by her brother, Perry." Franklin quickly tapped on Perry's name with his right index finger, his sign of conviction. Then went to the "Corporate Filings" search box, which included a side box with "Corporate Name" and one with "Person Name."

He typed in Perry Shorter's name in the latter box, then clicked for the search. It brought up seven company IDs, but no Classic Antiques. Scanning the companies, he chose the vague title of Impact Finance Corp, clicking on it. Only one name appeared on the corporate listing—an attorney, Jarvis Pickens—cited as the corporation's registrant. No listing of corporate officers or executives.

In a separate window, back to Google. Franklin typed in "Impact Finance Corporation Far River". A page of links appeared, the first an article with a headline "Impact Finance Hosts Chamber Membership Drive". Within the story Franklin found basic press-release style quotes from Impact Finance's chairman: Perry Shorter.

The following stories showed Impact purchasing and selling small businesses, nothing major. No listing of Classic Antiques.

To the other window and the Corporate Name box. He typed in "Impact Finance Corporation." He went to the corp's financial statements, clicking on the most recent year. The figures showed the handful of purchases and sales, but the bottom line showed a profit of only $100,000. Franklin decided Shorter must be the only executive involved in the corporate operations. Small change, really.

Franklin leaned back, thought, then googled Classic Antiques. Only a couple of items appeared, one an address and phone number, the other a simple listing with other antique stores. He double-checked the corporate filings site, this time writing in Classic Antiques. No go. So it wasn't incorporated.

"Jose, at City Hall, what's the direct line for the Business Permits Office?"

Jose provided, and Franklin dialed.

"Business Permits," answered the soft female voice.

"This is Reeves Franklin at the *Ledger* …"

"Whoa! I read your annexation story. Could have been more positive."

"Sorry. I'm out of the old 'Dragnet' school: Just the facts. And speaking of facts, could you check on a business permit for Classic Antiques."

"Classic Antiques … Classic Antiques …" Her voice sounded like a seductive radio ad for Viagra. "Naw, nothing here. What's the address?"

"Old Farm Road."

"That's in the county."

Franklin winced. He must be slipping. Of course it is.

"I knew that," he said with self-deprecating irritation. "Why did I call you?"

"Maybe it's fate," the Viagra voice responded.

"Sorry to waste your time. Thanks."

"Any time."

Hmmm, Franklin thought, then silently hung up the phone.

He looked up Luke Whitman's office number on his personal directory, then dialed his direct line.

"This is Luke."

"This is Reeves."

"Eww, the press. I have no comment."

"You're a lawyer."

"I'm an attorney."

"Okay. You know an attorney named Jarvis Pickens?"

"Now! He's a lawyer!"

"I see he's the registrant for a corporation called …"

"… Impact Finance. His only client."

"Really."

"Yep. Gives him a pretty nice living."

"But … I'm looking at their financial statement for last year. Only made just over a hundred grand."

"That's profit. Does it show the total income and expenses?"

"Ah … Ahhh. One point two million and one point one million. No itemizing."

"Salaries?"

"Only one line: One person, "Chief Executive", $250,973."

"That's Perry Shorter."

"And who's Perry Shorter?"

"Just a businessman."

"He's not your client, Luke. Who is he really?"

"Well, if you asked anybody in politics, they'd tell you he's the main fundraiser for Storm Weber."

"The mayor."

"The same."

"Hmmm. Okay. Thanks for the info."

"I don't know what you mean. I haven't even talked to you."

"Bye."

Click.

Franklin sat and thought. Then back to the computer search, where he called up the web page for the *Kansas City Star.* At its search window he wrote in "Terrence Farrow." Small stories of his being nabbed but never convicted.

Then Franklin wrote in the search window "Kansas City jewel thefts". A string of links. He clicked and read them one by one. After about a dozen, he opened a story about a major jewel heist from a KC millionaire's home. There were photos of the jewels which had been stolen. And in the third photo, there it was: The necklace Franklin had admired on Penny Shorter's delicate neck. He bookmarked the story, leaned back, and huffed a sigh.

Now the investigation would have to wait a day. So would the return call to the Mayor. Franklin needed to grab his paycheck and head home. He shouldn't have stayed this long.

Back at the townhouse, he trotted upstairs to the bedroom closet, pulled out the small chest, extracted the laptop, sat on the bed, activated the screen, and dove deep.

He found a blinking message from Viper. He clicked on it.

"Taipan: Black Mamba reports days of relentless observance. No sign of danger. No strangers. Only a handful of individuals met and welcomed by your daughter and her friend. I called him off, but he's determined to stay a couple of more days to make sure. So she's in good hands until mid-week. But seems at peace."

"Viper: Grateful. More than you know. To you and Black Mamba. As always, yell as required."

"Taipan: Only if dire. Out."

Franklin returned the laptop to its concealment and went to his PC. His heart ached, praying for his daughter. Then for her boyfriend, and especially her two protectors.

Then, feeling the urge, he called up a blank document and began to write.

After his unmeasured span in the space-time continuum, he re-read the writing, performed minor editing, nodded approval and thanked the Muse, then called up his email. He wrote Evelyn.

"Hello, my dear daughter. Trusting all is well there. All calm here. My two assailants scurried out of state. Authorities searching for them. No doubt will find them. Meanwhile, on we go. And I've written you a sonnet, which is attached. Love. And Love …"

He added the attachment, reading the poem one more time before sending:

Gentle Soul, Stay Gentle

Gentle soul, stay gentle through your currents,
your seeming endless storms. Breathe deep, convert
each fearful vision through prayer to advents
of peaceful imagery: angels' concerts,
loved ones gathered on smooth lake's sunset shore.
Know when Van Gogh painted his "Starry Night
Over the Rhone" he lighted it for your
eyes, your gentle soul. When Chopin takes flight,

glides through peaceful preludes, he's caressing
you. Listen to Whitman speak his poems
of joy, witnessing it, hearing it sing
in life's each moment—those calling anthems
seeking your response. When the Buddha strolled
his Eightfold Path, he knew your gentle soul.

~

In a couple of hours she would write back two brief sentences:

"Face rain. Love you."

That was enough.

~

Franklin called Cassie. Encouraged her to stay secluded a couple of more days, then return. She said she would, but Jackie was on her way back, wanting to work.

He decided to briefly drop by The Caboose, where the *Ledger* faithful would now be gathering.

Arriving, he went to the bar, ordering a seltzer and slice of lime. As the barkeep concurred, a strange voice intervened:

"Mr. Franklin?"

Reeves turned, finding a young man, probably in his mid-thirties. He eerily felt he had seen him before, but it wasn't clicking.

"I hear you have quite a jump shot."

It clicked. He was looking at an old teammate and yet wasn't.

"If you're Russell Page, you're a scientific wonder. You

don't age."

"I'm Russell Junior," the man said, smiling.

They shook hands, Franklin noting the fellow's strong grip.

"I was in memory shock for a couple of seconds," Franklin said with a grin.

"Daddy says you were a great teammate."

"It was easy to be with him. He loved to rebound and pass me the ball. And he had this nasty habit of strong-arming anyone who tried to deck me."

"That's him all right!" Junior laughed, then grew more solemn. "I recognized you and wanted to come over. I want to apologize."

"What for?"

"I'm a police officer. I gotta tell you, we were pretty embarrassed with what happened to you. There are good guys … and gals … on the force. We care about this city and its citizens. But there are also a few thugs. And now and then we have to weed out criminals, like this time. I gotta tell you, after I read your news article, I got so pis … excuse me … I got so angry …."

"Pissed will work," Franklin said with just a bit of a grin. Junior didn't grin.

"Well … okay … I got so pissed I got in my car and drove from home to the station, even went in to the chief's office. He was pissed too. And I guarantee you, we'll find those two guys and bring 'em to justice … Although I gotta tell you … from looking at the photo in the paper, you did a pretty good job of strong-arming yourself. They looked pretty beat up."

"Caught 'em by surprise is all."

Junior involuntarily laughed out loud, then caught himself.

"Uh … right." He grew quiet for a moment, his eyes actually hinting at tears.

"Anyway, sir. I want you to know, the word's out around the department. We gotta find out what went on with this shooting. And with what happened to you and Mr. Salisbury."

"Careful, Russell," Franklin deadpanned. "You keep calling Salsy 'Mr. Salisbury,' he's gonna strut into the paper and ask for a raise. Maybe even an editor's job."

Another involuntary laugh, followed by quiet. Then: "I also complained to my dad, who was glad to hear me say so. He was irate. And, uh, he said if I do run into you, to tell you take it easy, 'but keep full court pressin.'"

"Please tell him I said to keep rebounding. And thank you very much for coming up and speaking with me. I really appreciate it."

The young man smiled, turned a bit red, nodded, and walked away, back to a table where a lovely young woman was sitting alone, looking concerned as he returned. They spoke briefly, then she smiled and looked over at Franklin. He smiled and nodded toward them. Then turned and joined the *Ledger* domain.

Salsy wasn't there, evidently still working on a story for the next day. Franklin only stayed a few minutes, then he and his Toyota travelled to a meeting at the Grace Place. More settled after an hour of honesty, he returned to his townhouse, catching the local university's men's basketball game on television. They won. They seemed to win a lot lately, making it easier to watch. Then he grabbed a copy of W.H. Auden's collected poems and began reading.

7

"MAN IN RAIN"

Sitting alone in his living room, slouching in his favorite chair, he whispered the first line of Auden's "Miranda:" "My dear one is mine as mirrors are lonely …"

That was enough to surge him back to Melissa, Evelyn's mother. They had met during the late '60s, both working full-time summer jobs in the county clerk's office, filling out and mailing property re-evaluation statements to the county's residential and commercial property owners. He was about to finish college. She had a year left in high school. But they bonded psychically, both sharing weird and quick senses of humor, and a warm physical attraction.

Over the next couple of years they would stay in touch as she went to college and Franklin entered the army, knowing he would eventually test Vietnam. When he anonymously gravitated from the Army to the special, secret Marine outfit, his letters stopped flowing to Melissa's mailbox. She sadly decided he had lost interest.

Then three years later, he appeared at her apartment door in Dallas, where she had migrated across states for her first post-college job, adjusting claims for an insurance company. They both felt their fractured selves now were melding into a mended, inspiring whole.

They married, moved back to Far River, where Franklin joined the *Ledger* and Melissa decided to start law school, pausing only briefly to bear Evelyn. They were excitedly moving forward, feeling they were rightfully pursuing dreams and fulfilling talents, parenting a beautiful, gifted child, gathering with friends experiencing like challenges and satisfactions.

But the bliss of home life and hard work for the couple gradually began to dissolve. Franklin had always been haunted by deep fears he couldn't comprehend, and wouldn't express. Those now were further inflamed by his former secret, violent military life. He began drinking heavier and heavier, growing more silent and morose.

Melissa focused on trying to accept his constant series of isolation and morbidity. But he eventually began blacking out from drinking, growing violent both at home, and sometimes away from home at parties with friends. They began being invited to fewer functions. Then twice Franklin woke from blackouts at home to learn he had broken furniture and twice hit his wife, bruising her face each time.

He was mortified, filled with shame, terrified how he could have killed her had his blows been focused, which drunkenness—and now a higher power, he believed—disallowed. He went to see a psychiatrist, who then encouraged Melissa to come, and both joined a couples group being engrained with Eric Byrnes's transactional analysis, trying to cite and categorize their thoughts, feelings, and actions as child, adult, or parent.

It seemed to briefly help. But then Franklin fell to the drink's craving, and Melissa had suffered enough.

"Either you have to move out, or Evelyn and I are moving," she demanded.

He moved out to a cheap, dark, sullen apartment downtown close to the newspaper. Divorce followed, combined with scheduled custody days with Evelyn. And Melissa's constant pleadings to pay child support, a feeble responsibility to one whose involuntary top priority is alcohol.

After two years of progressive descent, he decided to move to the Northeast, what the sober crew calls a "geographic cure:" "I know: I'll move to another city! Then I'll get my life together and be happy forever!" It never works.

What *did* work for a while: Stumbling into both a job and a lover on the Jersey Shore near Manhattan.

Franklin had wandered his way to Loch Haven, a township about an hour by car from New York. He had picked up a part-time job taking orders and operating the cash register at a little independent sub sandwich shop, and also began writing freelance articles for *The Sand Dune*, a local Shore weekly. And he was consistently writing poetry.

His creative writing led him to research in the local college library. And it was there he linked up with Laura.

Franklin was seated at one of the long mahogany tables in the library's literature section, diving into writing a poem after reading a selection of Robert Lowell's verse. As he scribbled a line, he suddenly heard a soft yet firm voice.

"One dark night,
my Tudor Ford climbed the hill's skull …"

His focus bothered, Franklin looked up to see a slender blond woman, her blue eyes aimed at the Lowell book resting by his elbow. She was smiling slightly, and turned her gaze to his eyes as she continued:

"I watched for love-cars. Lights turned down,
they lay together, hull to hull,
where the graveyard shelves on the town. . . .
My mind's not right …"

~

She stopped there. They stared at each other like old friends who have stumbled on one another. But they weren't old friends. They were strangers met up in the sacred sanctuary of books.

"I'm Laura Blevins," she said softly.

Then they were sipping coffee in the student center,

not talking about themselves, but about Lowell: his penitent New England penchant for understatement, his alcoholism, his dear yet destructive relationship with the brilliant Jean Stafford.

"I heard him read in Manhattan a couple of years before he died," Laura said, her eyes looking past Franklin, past the student center, past the Jersey Shore to that crowded gathering at New York University's auditorium. "He had this uncanny ability. He'd be reading his poem aloud, then stop and make a comment to further clarify, or perhaps fill us in on a relationship, then read a while longer, then interrupt again, then read. But it was all so natural. You'd think it would irritate the audience. But it just drew us in closer to him … as if we all were the poem."

Franklin was gazing at her, lost in her eyes and voice. Eventually he realized she had stopped talking, and was simply staring at him, smiling.

"You sound like a Southerner, Reeves," she said, wanting to turn the attention to him. "How did you come to the Shore?"

Franklin didn't want to go there.

"Tell me more about Lowell," he said. "In his photos he seems gaunt, almost sickly."

"The older photos, yeah. The drinking was getting to him. But he was thin, even when younger.

"What about his voice, his reading?"

Laura looked back at the distant auditorium, recalling.

"You know, his voice was soft, seeming almost a whisper. So personal. Without the microphone, the first row might not have heard him. But we all *did* hear him. I was near the middle of the auditorium. But it was like he was right next to me. And it wasn't just the physical sound. It was the poem itself. And it was him."

They would end up having dinner together. Then agreeing to another dinner and movie that weekend. By the movie's end, walking the boardwalk together, gazing out at the dark Atlantic and the sea of stars, Franklin finally felt free enough to talk about growing up in Far River. Of Melissa and Evelyn. Of the sudden decision to move East.

Dr. Laura Blevins listened closely to every word. The day they met, he had learned of her growing up in Indiana. Of her earning a PhD in English literature. Of her joy of teaching and her own writing.

She had spoken over that first dinner of her most recent book, an analysis of Emily Dickinson's poetry. Then backed off, seeing in Franklin's eyes an unease, as if her accomplishments were a threat to him. She had tried again to ask about his background, but he had deflected it, returning her to the great New England poet's life. She had decided to respect his privacy, and his willingness to hear more about literature.

But she was very pleased that this evening boardwalk stroll had opened him up. And she was sensitive to his obvious pain at the broken marriage, at having moved halfway across America, abandoning his life in Far River, and his daughter.

"Oh … hell …" Franklin suddenly realized, stopping and staring out at the ocean's dark. "I … I deserted her, didn't I?"

"Your daughter?"

"Yeah."

"Aren't you communicating with her?"

Franklin was silent, staring out. Laura watched him a long moment, honoring his silence.

Then she said, "Why don't you send her some poetry?"

Franklin turned and looked at her. Tears gleamed in his eyes.

"Send her some poetry," he echoed.

"Yes. Isn't that the best of you?"

"Yeah … Yeah, I guess it is."

They smiled at each other, turned and continued to walk. Laura slipped her right arm into his left and pushed close to him.

At the door of her simple brick home close to campus, she invited him in. But he wasn't ready for that. In another week, he would be. In three months, he had moved in with her.

For six months, life, love, and literature flourished. Franklin worked hard, very hard, to not drink, and to control it when he did, particularly at faculty parties. And there were a lot of faculty parties.

After six months, and the start of a new fall semester,

the old fears, the secret past, the shame of leaving his daughter, the sense of unfulfillment with low-skilled part-time work and dead-end freelance writing … it all became too much.

The bender led him to disappear for a week. When he returned to Loch Haven, the freelance work was gone, and Laura was deeply concerned.

"Why did you leave?" she asked.

"I had to. I'm not safe to be around when I'm drunk."

"Where did you go?"

"Down the Shore a ways. To Long Branch. Got a cheap motel room. And just drank. Don't know how long. Don't remember much."

"A week."

That's all she said. She left to teach a class.

His first night back was marred with muteness. After apologizing, he could think of nothing else to say. She refused to preach, or to hammer him with her worry, and she was too emotional to offer any constructive solution.

The next morning after breakfast, Laura gently confronted him.

"I have a couple of friends who couldn't stop drinking," she said, her voice calm, caring. "They went to Alcoholics Anonymous. They don't drink now. Their lives are full."

Franklin stayed silent. They were sitting on the den couch, and he was staring at the painting on the wall across from them: a black-and-gray oil on white canvas created by

Laura's friend Tony Del Rio, chair of the art department. It was called *Man in Rain*, a torrent of slashing dark strokes, so thick they glared off the surface. At first glance, the deluge seemed all there was. But when the eyes focused deeper, the slightest image of a hunched over human figure became visible. At this specific instant, that suffering shape was all Franklin could see.

He felt he was running out of time, out of breath, out of life. He turned and gazed at Laura. His distorted face suddenly tortured her. Tears formed in her eyes. She let out a muffled breath and fell into his arms. They remained there for what seemed a hushed eon.

"Why don't you go see Doc?" she said, her voice so soft it seemed from another life.

Two days later, Franklin was on the train to Manhattan and an appointment with Doc Hatfield at his Midtown Restoration Center. As a young doctor of physical therapy, Roland Hatfield had become deeply frustrated with medical surgeons and their lack of care for patients after cutting and sewing them up, sending them out without rehabilitation. He decided to change that. First he returned to school, earned a doctor of psychology degree, studied yoga, then analyzed a bevy of weight and exercise programs, including those used by international Olympic trainers.

Back in Manhattan, he melded all this into his own treatment program; became the mentor, savior really, for professional ballet dancers. After their misguided dedication led them to starve themselves and stay thin, they'd suffer deep muscle and ligament injuries at the hands of abusive choreographers, then limp from the stage, believing their careers … their lives … were over. Then one turned up at the Restoration Center. Then another. Eventually a human stream developed, and Doc Hatfield had become a legend in the international world of ballet. He also treated others who were physically ill, from actors and athletes to business people.

Doc would bring in the broken-down human, immediately put him or her on a flow chart—a daily listing of everything put into the body, and the time. He would turn that around into a proper diet of lean meat and fish, and trove of vegetables and fruits; and water, always water throughout the day and night.

At the same time, he would start the wounded on the basic motions of his weight-lifting and exercise program, a combination of yoga's deep breathing with systematic body movements. It centered on a straightened spine, and using the legs rather than back when lifting weight. The order was to "pinch and extend:" pinch the buttocks, then extend the spine.

"Envision the neck's brief dent at the back base of the skull," Doc would direct. "Pretend it's attached to a hook, with the hook linked to a cable stretching to the ceiling. The cable pulls the body toward heaven, straightening the spine and, in turn, placing all the body's organs in proper alignment."

Simple but not easy. Yet the vital key to physical restoration.

The third prong of Restoration—after diet and exercise—involved private sessions with Doc in his office. He would begin to lovingly invade the psyche, eventually convincing the suffering of their true value as humans. They'd begin to understand their actual needs, desires, and talents. After a while, the holistic three-pronged process would not only heal them, it would inspire them to attain truly fulfilled lives.

Laura had met Doc through the college's basketball coach, who had gone to Doc as an injured outstanding collegian. Doc's care had not only sent him back into competition, it had affected his philosophy of play, and eventually of coaching and living. Coach had recommended Doc when Laura had ruptured her shoulder lifting weights.

Laura in turn introduced Franklin to Doc. The couple would make the hour-long drive into Manhattan two or three times a week to work out. Doc obviously loved Laura, and he liked Franklin, saw the potential that the younger man did not yet see. But Franklin was faithful to the workouts, and focused on perfection. And, while this didn't stop his drinking, it did lessen the physical destruction of the addiction, allowing Franklin's body to bounce back quickly following a bad night. But it had also enabled Laura to hold on to hope that Franklin might eventually see the light and stop imbibing altogether. He couldn't.

On the train ride in, Franklin was feeling relieved. He decided he could manipulate the situation now. Move away from Laura's suggestion of AA, and get Doc to take care of him. Laura would like that, and it might give Franklin some wiggle room.

In Doc's small office, seated on the other side of the desk, hugging one of the two comfy visitor chairs, Franklin looked sincerely at his therapist.

"I need to stop drinking," he said solemnly.

Air filled Doc's barrel chest as he leaned back in his padded swivel chair. His powerful gaze lasered in on Franklin, measuring his friend's sincerity. Then he slowly raised his cleanly shaved head and face toward the ceiling, gently lifted both strong hands as in grateful prayer. Held there a moment. Then lowered his arms again and stared at Franklin, the slightest smile on his face.

"You remember a while back … I sat alone with you and said, 'I don't want to come to your funeral, baby.'"

"I remember."

Doc studied him a bit longer, then added flatly, "I've dealt with people for decades with this problem … You need to go to AA."

Fuck.

Franklin thought it. He didn't say it aloud. Here he had come to Doc to take care of him, but the guru had cornered him the same way Laura was trying to.

Eventually, after a couple of years sober, Franklin would figure out Doc *was* taking care of him. He was telling him the truth. The disease was lying to him, so he couldn't clearly see that at the time.

He would begin going to AA meetings for nine months, three or four a week, but not take the basic suggestions: ninety meetings in ninety days. Get a sponsor. Work the Twelve Steps. And keep moving forward.

He told himself that daily meetings were impossible. He didn't trust folks enough to get a sponsor. And the Steps seemed to be orders rather than suggestions, especially what he saw as a mandate to believe in God.

During the nine months, he began to find freelance work in Manhattan, would travel into town three days a week to interview sources for stories. He'd also work out at Restoration before returning to Laura on the Shore.

But after nine months, he slid off the Friday night train at the Shore. He was only a block from the favorite sports bar. He felt exhausted, and his disease reasoned that a brief visit to see the old gang, catch up while he sipped on a "nonalcoholic" beer, would be a very human, friendly thing to do.

Six nonalcoholic beers later, he began to feel uncomfortable, and left. Within two days he was drinking again, first beer, then pre-meal beer, wine with the meal, and brandy after. Then doing that every day, and obsessing about drinking when he wasn't downing a brew or other poison.

In his mind, Laura seemed to be fine with it. But she

wasn't. After two months, she slapped him with reality.

"I'm in love with someone else," she said at the end of a boardwalk stroll.

"You … don't love me anymore?"

"Yes, I love you, Reeves. But you're a drunk. We'll never have a true relationship as long as you're a drunk. And you know that."

Yes. He did know that. Her honesty made him admit it.

He sheepishly moved out, to a small rotgut room on top of The Anchor Pub, a hundred-year-old stable two blocks from the ocean.

Then it seemed clear to him: He could go back to AA, and later, he could get Laura back.

He didn't get her back. But he got a sponsor, began working the Steps with him, attended daily meetings. He began to get sober, then live sober.

These memories had flooded through Franklin for only a few moments. But the process had exhausted him. He fell back in his chair, closed his eyes, and began breathing deeply. He fell asleep, waking to realize it was daylight outside.

The memories had stirred his subconscious, leading him to dream. On awaking, it led him to write.

BLURRED RAPIDS

In my dream, the small white house with oyster-
shell roof—chimney waving ghostly signal

to me—rests on emerald grass, moisture
feeding it from the wide river, ripples
and rapids blurring before me like some
dream within the dream. I'm on the other
side, gazing across fertile valley—home
from war, yet still not home—my dead brother's
whisper urging me on: *Tell them the truth*,
he rasps. *Don't let them get away with it.*
My jaw's clinched so tight, I feel a weak tooth
chip, drooling out along my lips. I spit
it toward the far mountain. Hear my harsh hiss
repeat, *Don't dare let them see you like this.*

~

He wouldn't show it to anyone.

8

HIDING IN PLAIN SIGHT

FOLLOWING HIS MONDAY MORNING WORKOUT at the Pump Station, Franklin sallied into the *Ledger*, timing his visit for after the city-edition deadline, when Ray Perry would be free to talk. He plopped in the chair next to Perry's desk, waiting for the city editor to unglue his eyes from the computer monitor. Eventually, Perry's focus turned to Franklin.

"I want $1,000 for a story," Franklin said bluntly.

Perry lurched, frowned, and snarled, "You want me to pay you what!?!"

"No no," Franklin responded, shaking his head and raising a hand. "I don't want you to *pay* me that for a story. I need $1,000 so I can follow through on a story. Money to make a buy."

Perry's face looked as if a physician had demanded he

endure a hemorrhoid operation.

"What!?!"

"Look, Ray. You know the stories we've run on the police assassination. You know Salsy's latest story, his unnamed source saying the police had set up the robber, who was actually a jewel thief."

"Yes. I do."

"I believe I've found the fence here in Far River."

Whenever the potential of a front-page lead story ignited Ray Perry's journalistic soul, his eyes would take on a Hannibal Lecter glare. This was one of those times.

"I saw the stolen necklace at the antique store I included in my annexation story. And get this: It's owned by a guy named Perry Shorter, a major fundraiser for the mayor."

The editor's mouth slowly widened like a lustful Mr. Hyde.

"How'd you know the necklace was stolen?"

"I found a burglary story in the *Kansas City Star*. There was a photo of the necklace. Same one the sales woman at the antique store was wearing. And there's a glass case of jewelry there, too. I'm betting all hot."

"There on display?"

"Hiding in plain sight."

Perry glared out into the distance, his inner computer rattling.

"C'mon," Perry said, rising from his chair. "Let's go talk to Shelby."

Prescott Shelby was the *Ledger*'s publisher and editor-in-chief. The fourth generation of Shelbys to hold that title, and the purse strings. Franklin updated him on the police assassination story, and his linking the antique store to the stolen necklace.

"I want to buy the necklace, get the receipt, bring both back and photograph them," Franklin told his audience of two. Perry and Shelby looked at each other.

"Whatta you think, Prescott?" Perry asked.

The publisher studied Franklin.

"Why don't you buy the necklace yourself, get the receipt, and we'll reimburse you," countered Shelby. Newspaper publishers were known to possess a genetic Scrooge defect, and Shelby shared it.

"I thought about that," Franklin said smoothly. "If I purchase the necklace on my own, I'm basically buying known stolen property. But if it's the newspaper's money, done with your approval for the specific purpose of unveiling the fencing operation …"

"That's good!" piped in Perry, suddenly taking Franklin's side for the first time. "Prescott, that's a good plan."

Shelby gritted his teeth.

"Okay," he huffed. "I'll make it happen. I'll have the cash for you tomorrow."

The next afternoon, Franklin's Toyota was making its way back along Old Farm Road. Rain, mixed with sleet, pelted the windshield, making it difficult to see, even with the new wiper blades swiping away. Lightning flashed like stark memory, suddenly shocking Franklin's intense recall.

~

1974. Two days of heavy tropical rains were flooding the downstream areas of Kuala Lumpur. Franklin had been shipped from Vietnam across the South China Sea to Malaysia, then sped by chopper and dropped in the rain forest just outside the Malay capital. He had to find a single hut on the Gombak River. Rubah's hut. Rubah—the Malay word for "fox" or "foxy." The nickname American military intelligence had given for Malaysia's slippery Communist assassin.

Earlier, the CIA had received a report that Rubah was planning to murder Francis T. Underhill, Jr., the U.S. ambassador to Malaysia. And within a day, Franklin had been called before his commander at Da Nang, provided photos of Rubah, a couple of helicopter shots of his hut, details of the foxy one's preferred weapons, methods of attack, fighting style, even name and a photo of his lover. Then Franklin was immediately driven to his ship and was gone. He didn't even ask why the CIA wasn't handling it. Then he thought, maybe they were. War at times seemed to meld military and spy operations.

The spy photos had aligned Rubah's hut with a trio of snowy-orchid trees that had grown together, winding up over the hut's rear like an emerald and white cape. Franklin had spent four hours slipping among trees along the river's shore, searching, then spotting it. He smiled briefly, considering the irony of flora rising in a tropical forest's humidity, but somehow named "snowy-orchid."

His eyes canvassed the surroundings, looking for a tree he might climb to get a better view for a rifle shot. But the rain wasn't letting up, and he decided to sneak in close, hide in the vegetation, and wait to see if his target might appear.

He lost track of time, focused so keenly on the hut he no longer felt the torrent soaking him. His orders were to get in fast, get out fast. Rubah would soon be moving to make his kill.

Then a man's head eked out of the hut's door, eyes wincing, checking the downpour, then just as quickly disappearing back inside the hut. Rubah.

Franklin reacted in an instant, running toward the hut, his right hand pulling his Glock 19 pistol from its holster, his left hand sliding the fighting knife from its scabbard. He knew Rubah worked alone, but in his hut he might not be alone.

Pushing rapidly through the thin wooden door, Franklin crouched low, eyes alert to any movement. Rubah had heard him enter and was reaching for his automatic weapon on the near table. As he grabbed it and turned toward Franklin, a bullet hit the Malaysian in the forehead, another pierced his left eye, and a third split his lips and teeth, carrying through and out the rear of the skull.

Suddenly Franklin sensed motion to his left. He

turned just as a woman was screaming, swiping at him with a knife. He pirouetted away, her blade barely slicing his left shoulder. But she had opened herself, and Franklin's knife blade gouged deep into her throat, his strength lifting her upon her toes, then six inches off the floor. He held her there for a heartbeat, then jerked back on the knife, the bloody blade ejecting from her as she crumpled to the dirty rug, body helplessly shaking.

Franklin swiftly stepped to Rubah's body, not to check his wounds, but to add two bullets into his skull. He fired two more bullets into the woman's forehead to end her suffering. Then he exited the hut, heading upriver and to his assigned meeting place where the chopper would rendezvous and carry him back to the ship.

Ambassador Underhill would never know this happened.

~

The journalist's Toyota pulled up in front of the antique store. He sat still for a few moments, deep breathing, praying. Then he reached over to his athletic bag, pulled out a towel, wiped the sweat from his face. He gazed in the rear-view mirror at his eyes, urging them back to the present. Then he got out and trotted through the rain to the shop's front door.

The frozen pelting outside had kicked up the heat inside, forcing a more stifling, musty aroma than on his previous visit. He stood alone in the shop, waiting for the irresistible Penny Shorter to appear. Soon she stepped from the back room, but not the same perky, smiling fashion model who had amazed him earlier. She suddenly stopped on seeing Franklin, mouthing a dull, "Oh … It's you."

She moved behind the counter, trying to act busy. She was nervous, not sure what to do. Franklin walked to the counter and watched her. She seemed to be avoiding eye contact, her head down, shuffling through papers. He stood silent, patient.

Finally she looked up. Her flowing red hair fell partially over her left eye and jaw. But something was wrong. Franklin saw hints of puffiness in her cheek; and makeup tried to cover, but couldn't completely disguise, a black left eye.

"How are you, Penny?" Franklin asked, almost deadpanned.

"I shouldn't talk to you," she responded, her voice shaky.

"What's wrong? I misquote you in the annexation story?"

She looked him straight in the eye. Tears were starting to form.

"You need to go," she blurted.

"What's going on?"

"I've got nothing to say."

Franklin studied her. She wasn't wearing an expensive necklace, no fancy rings. He looked over at the glass case. It was empty.

His eyes returned to Penny's. She looked quickly down, shuffling through more papers.

"What happened to the jewelry?" Franklin asked calmly. "I really liked it, especially the necklace you were wearing when I interviewed you. I wanted to buy something for my girlfriend."

Penny glared up at him, then back down at the papers.

"I've got nothing to say," she snapped.

"I can guess why," Franklin said smoothly, almost in a croon. "Your brother read our stories about the police murdering that Kansas City jewel thief …."

The redhead's eyes lurched back into his.

"… Then he saw my annexation story, and that you had talked to me …"

Her eyes blazed tears. If she had a weapon, he might have a problem, Franklin thought. But she didn't.

"He have a temper, your brother?"

"The sonuvabitch!" she growled. "I've done nothing but take care of this store. He knows that."

Franklin studied her. That fear and anger were aimed more toward her brother, not the guy standing in front of her.

"The fencing operation won't last much longer," Franklin said, his voice growing softer, like an understanding friend. "We're on to it. The cops are on to it. The prosecuting attorney's on to it. Since the stolen jewels crossed state lines, no doubt the FBI's on to it now."

That power list broke her. She began sobbing, leaning over the counter, fingers clawing at the glass top.

"No doubt they'll come here before long," Franklin advised even more softly.

"I didn't know the jewels were stolen," Penny whimpered. "I didn't know …."

Franklin let her cry, and waited. Eventually the weeping ebbed. An open box of tissues sat on the counter's far corner. He retrieved the box, flipped out the top kerchief and handed it to her. She took it, wiped her eyes, blew her nose. Silence for a full minute.

"Then he brought that guy in one day …." she murmured.

"Who brought in what guy?"

"Perry … he came in with that guy … in your article. I saw his picture … and realized it was him …."

"You mean Terrence Farrow … the jewel thief?"

"Yeah."

"When was that?"

"About a week … before ….

"Before he was shot?"

"Yeah." A sudden blurt of crying. Franklin waited. Then silence again.

"But you didn't know who he was?"

"I'd never seen him before. They just came in quickly, looked over the jewels in the display case … spoke so softly to each other I couldn't hear. I figured it was a potential buyer. Then I walked over and introduced myself to him, irked that Perry hadn't been courteous to me. But the name he gave me wasn't the one you used in the paper. Said his name was … Smith. Yeah … right …."

She gave a brief gallows smile. Then slowly shook her head "no," as if this all couldn't be real.

Franklin studied her closely.

"Might be better if you get out of here," Franklin suggested. "My experience is … someone's deciding about now that you're a danger they can't afford."

Penny gazed at him, fear growing in her eyes.

"You need to go to the FBI. I'm not sure right now who you could trust at the local police."

"W … will … you take me?"

The rain had eased as they drove back into Far River. Neither one spoke for the first five miles. Then:

"How'd you do that?" Penny asked softly. "Those two cops who attacked you?"

"You mean the parking-lot caper?" Franklin almost whispered, his mouth corners hinting at an ironic grin.

"Yeah. They could have killed you. Couldn't they?"

"They were pushy, showed weapons, but talked a lot. Probably weren't planning on shooting."

"But you took their guns away? How'd you do that?"

"Caught 'em by surprise, I guess."

Silence. Franklin turned and looked at her. She was watching him, a smile of admiration more in her eyes than on her lips.

"Think maybe you should call the FBI? Let 'em know we're coming?" she asked.

"Don't carry a phone."

"What?"

"I'm still a landline guy."

"Seriously?"

"Not too seriously. But factually, yeah."

"Everybody's got a smartphone these days. Keeps them from building relationships."

Her voice was sounding lighter. She was feeling safer.

"I figure if the NSA or other fed agencies … or the local gendarme want to tap me, they'll have to do it on my landline and email. But if they want to follow my every move … they'll need to do it by spy satellite … not smartphone."

She snorted a brief laugh. Then, "What about the FBI? They're a fed agency. But you trust them?"

"Beggars, as they say, can't be uppity."

Franklin again looked at her. She was looking straight ahead, smiling. Then she laid her head back on the seat's headrest, and closed her eyes.

"We could use my phone," she said softly.

"They're more impressed when you enter their fortress and press flesh. Let's do that."

They did do that. When they walked through the FBI's door on the downtown federal building's third floor, the receptionist perked up when Franklin introduced himself.

"So that's you," she said smiling. "How'd you do that to those two undercover cops?"

"We need to speak to the agent covering the case regarding the murdered jewel thief, Terrence Farrow," Franklin responded effortlessly, his confidential smile leading the receptionist to giggle, then grow serious as she called an agent.

"I'll get Senior Special Agent Simpson," she said.

A calm, straight-faced African American, Simpson proved no-nonsense, which was just what Franklin expected. Simpson listened to Franklin's information, then questioned Penny Shorter. Satisfied with her answers, he told her he was preparing protection for her, including a living space where no one could reach her. Franklin studied her to see if she felt safe with that. The gratitude in her eyes showed she was. And he left her with Simpson.

"You're not going to write about this, are you?" Simpson queried forcefully.

"Thank you for helping her, Agent Simpson. And for your service."

That's all Franklin said. Then he turned and walked away.

Back at his townhouse, Franklin checked the mailbox. A small stack of envelopes with the usual utility bills and junk mail. Then, in the middle of the brief pack: a simple white envelope with no return address. Postmark Chicago.

He didn't open the envelope while outside. He entered

his townhouse, flopped in his favorite chair, placed the mail stack on the wooden TV tray beside him, and opened the anonymous letter.

Inside peeked a single sheet of folded white paper. He parted the fold to see a message of only two typed words:

Ranch Hand

Franklin stared at the note for a long moment, then rose and trotted upstairs to his bedroom.

As he unpacked and opened the laptop, he recalled his small assassins squad of Marine comrades in Vietnam. They had witnessed the last days of Operation Ranch Hand, the American military's massive defoliation program using Agent Orange. The program had deployed more than nineteen million gallons of the herbicide over four and a half million acres of land.

The massive poisoning damaged millions of Vietnamese as well as American military personnel, even genetically harming generations from both countries into the twenty-first century.

Franklin and Fitz had bitterly joked that karma would turn on the Americans one day. That the U.S. would suffer its own Operation Ranch Hand at home, perhaps a plague, perhaps a violent revolution. They didn't know when, but history shows destruction eventually comes to civilizations. "Ranch Hand" became their common term whenever they referred to epidemics or revolutions occurring in other countries.

Franklin and Fitz had used the term in New York during their last meeting. They still felt some major pandemic—disease or revolution in nature—might occur. Not knowing when, they still believed they should always strive for the greatest physical and psychological shape to survive it.

Now … this note in the mail. Franklin went deep into the Dark Web, came to the website, and found within it a specially encrypted message from Viper to Taipan:

Taipan: Enemy in your area on March 17. Are you willing to cleanse?

Franklin's body flinched. Viper knew he hadn't killed in decades; had no desire to kill again. If he's asking, he must feel Franklin would consider it his sworn duty to do so.

His mind began racing. "Ranch Hand" meant epidemic or violent revolution. The news had offered no warnings of any bug starting to spread across the country. But politically the country was heavily divided. And military circles, Franklin knew, would privately be sharing concern about the new inhabitants of the White House. While they welcomed the new president's desire to build the military budget, career officers and veterans had been extremely wary of his fascist leanings from the time he had announced his candidacy.

In these first months in office the new chief executive, who constantly emphasized his role as commander in chief, had begun revealing a more dangerous fascist agenda: threatening freedom of the press and expression at home, and calling for even heavier aggression against foreign nations, including the use of nuclear weapons. Much of the uneducated public felt the military would favor such a dictatorial approach, but Franklin through experience knew better. The military oath is to defend the Constitution. Not the president. Not the Congress. The Constitution. Against all enemies, domestic or foreign.

Now Viper was announcing revolution, apparently against a domestic enemy of the Constitution. A national enemy. But who? The White House? That was hundreds of miles from Far River. How could a specific enemy be here?

Leaving the laptop open, Franklin hurried from his bedroom into his writing room, sat at his PC and went to the *Ledger*'s online website. He called up the monthly Calendar of Events, went to the month of March, and scanned state activities for March 17—now a week away. Lots of St. Patrick's Day celebrations. The major university's basketball team was playing locally, its last regular-season game.

He looked under Organization Events. Normal drab stuff. Then, there in the middle: The state bar association annual meeting. Honors Dinner guest speaker: the Attorney General of the United States.

Franklin sat back, gazing out his writing room windows at the sunny afternoon fading to pre-dusk. The new Attorney General was about as fascist as they came: Old South, racist, law and order, including wanting to militarize state and local police. Would Viper consider him an enemy of the Constitution?

Yes.

Franklin strode back into the bedroom, sat at the laptop, and typed in his response:

Viper: Negative on cleansing. Discouraging any such action. Let the people rule.

He pressed the send button. He sat still, deep breathing, praying, needing to pray. After a long ten minutes, no reply. So he closed the laptop and returned it to its closet and box.

Downstairs, he selected Beethoven's *Ninth Symphony.* He needed its choral caress, its "Ode to Joy." He turned to go flop in his chair. Then, the sound of a key in the door, a click, and open.

Cassie stood there, smiling.

"She's baaaaack," she offered, softly mocking the little girl in Spielberg's *Poltergeist.*

Franklin moved to and enveloped her.

"Just in time," he said.

9

BINGO

FRANKLIN AND CASSIE DECIDED to take the next day off from writing and focus on each other. They traveled out of town an hour to Lake of Peace, the translated Indian name, a recreation area nearly uninhabited on this waning-winter day in midweek. Taking a boat ride, the whipping chilled air and pristine water seemed to calm the universe. They dined at a fancy seafood restaurant on the lakeshore. Then they returned to Far River and a rare weeknight together. Following Hemingway's advice, they made love as if they'd invented it.

The next morning, Franklin felt relaxed and strong gliding through his Australian crawl in the Pump Station pool. Then, during his shower—mind weaving between Viper's message and Penny Shorter's fearful eyes—he decided to make a brief research visit to the *Ledger*, then head to the mayor's office.

Back at the *Ledger*, he got Ray Perry to accompany him to Prescott Shelby's office where he returned Shelby's grand of green. Then he filled them in on the details through leaving Penny Shorter with the FBI. He would include that in a written story, but he wanted to visit the mayor first. The publisher and city editor, scenting blood in the water, urged him onward.

Seated at a Ledger computer, Franklin made a call.

"Luke Whitman."

"Reeves Franklin, Luke. You still pilot an airplane?"

"Why? You want to finally risk going up with me?"

"Not in this lifetime."

"I haven't flown in quite a while."

"You still up on FAA regs?"

"Gotta be."

"Does the FAA require passengers on private flights to be registered in some kind of log or record book? Wondering if I could find a couple of names who might have flown to a specific location on a certain day."

"You'll need to check the private company. They fly out of Far River?"

"Probably."

"This have anything to do with your earlier call to me? The mayor and Perry Shorter?"

"You should be an investigative reporter."

"Doesn't pay enough. Shorter has a plane. Housed at

Reavis Air. You might try there. Ask for Wells Lister. Tell him I suggested you call him."

"I thought I never talked to you."

"Wells is a good guy. Reavis has supported the mayor his entire tenure. But Wells's brother-in-law ran against Storm Weber last election. Wells believes the mayor stole the election from him. He never publicly voices that. But if he can anonymously sting the mayor, he probably will gently jump at the chance. Call him. Hold on …."

Luke looked up Lister's number at the airport and informed Franklin.

Lister was obliging. Franklin gave him a week of possible dates when Weber and Shorter might have flown to Kansas City, where Weber had purchased his fancy blue fedora. It didn't take long to find the flight on Lister's computer: February 15. Returned the seventeenth. Three passengers: Weber, Shorter, and a Travis Cooney. A fourth passenger joined them on the return trip, but the name wasn't on Lister's computer. It might be filed at the Kansas City airport.

Franklin thanked Lister, and called Luke again.

"Lister was very helpful," Franklin told the attorney. "A third name was listed with Weber and Shorter. A Travis Cooney. You know who that might be?"

"He's the assistant chief of police."

Bingo.

"So Cooney would have the extradition papers for

Terrence Farrow? A fourth passenger returned with them, but Lister didn't have the name on file. I'm betting it was Farrow."

"That would work," Luke said. "I'm betting they did it without the police chief knowing. Cooney's an old buddy of Weber's. A twenty-year veteran of the department. But the city board passed him over for chief. They wanted somebody from outside to come in and make changes. Both Weber and Cooney are still nursing grudges over that … I'd ask you what you're gonna do with that information, but …."

"You haven't talked to me." Franklin grinned. "You'll read about it."

"Look forward. Bye."

Franklin briefly reviewed his notes, then headed to City Hall.

Storm Weber's secretary Mona Goldstein was the spitting image of comedian Sarah Silverman, but with a softer voice and seductive smile. She said of course the mayor's schedule was packed, but she'd try to sneak Franklin in for a few minutes. She knew the mayor wanted to talk with him about his annexation story.

Fifteen minutes later, Franklin was seated in a side chair facing both the mayor's huge desk and the closed door to the reception area. The former assassin had long ago engrained the habit of never sitting with his back to the door. Ever since he was twelve, actually, after he read a *Classics Illustrated* comic book showing Wild Bill Hickok shot dead from behind with his back to the door, holding aces and eights, the Dead Man's Hand.

"First, Reeves, I want to say how sorry I am about the trouble you had with those two thug cops. I don't know how they got on the force. But we're gonna get to the bottom of that whole thing."

Politically wise of Weber to immediately bring that up, Franklin thought. But the reporter wasn't going to pursue that right now. He'd play low key and bide his time.

"Yeah, I'm still not sure what happened. How I was able to turn their assault around. I just feel lucky to be alive." He knew Weber knew he was lying, and that was fine. "And I'm sure Bart Salisbury will get to the bottom of it. He's a good reporter."

"Yes … he is," Weber said dully, as if pacing where to go next. Then his mood suddenly changed as he chided lightly, "Anyway, you coulda been more friendly to us in your annexation story."

"Couldn't put words in their mouths, mayor. I just asked straight questions and they gave straight answers."

"Far River needs that extra land for growth."

"Then I'd suggest you get out there and meet with them … like *they* suggested."

"We're planning to do just that. Take a look at this."

Weber rose and stepped to a giant map of the city which covered most of the wall behind Franklin, who rose to stand beside him.

"You see the city limits," Weber said, stretching his right arm and winding it around the city's outline. "We've been this size for forty years. The city's grown a lot, and the county area has been growing a helluva lot. They need city services."

"Yeah. I've read your annexation proposal."

"You see, Reeves, this could really be a boon to the tax base. When you consider …."

"Hey, Storm, sorry to interrupt. Mona had stepped out for coffee, and I wanted to …"

"Not now, Perry!" snapped a startled Weber.

Franklin turned toward the door. There stood Perry Shorter. Franklin had seen his photo in one of the newspaper articles he had researched. And now he saw an opening.

"Perry Shorter!" Franklin called with a grin, briskly moving toward him and offering a handshake.

Shorter took it, smiling, but not sure who he was meeting.

"Reeves Franklin with the *Ledger*," Franklin said, now smirking. He was holding the right hand that had given Penny Shorter a swollen jaw and black eye. A burning thought told him to break it, but his sober experience held him back. He simply shook it, then let go.

Blood was quickly draining from Shorter's face, realizing his greeter's identity.

"Glad you're here," Franklin said, taking the offensive. He moved to and pulled up a chair for Shorter. "Won't you join us? I've got a couple of questions for you and the mayor about the annexation area."

Weber let out an involuntary huff. Shorter reluctantly moved to the chair and sat. Franklin returned to his seat. Weber moved to and sat on his desk's edge close to Franklin.

"Now, look here, Reeves. Perry's got no connection to this annexation proposal."

"I think I see a connection," Franklin countered, "but you two need to clear it up for me. Because it's getting complicated."

He sat looking toward each of the men. They both stared at him solemnly.

"I'm wondering about a February 15 flight you two took to Kansas City. With the assistant chief of police."

His small audience looked like he'd sapped all oxygen from the room. And now he'd test them.

"And the three of you flying back on February 17 with Terrence Farrow."

Silence. Then Weber's hollow voice:

"This interview's over. Now."

Franklin didn't stop. And he wanted to make clear to them he wasn't alone in his pursuing them.

"The way we figure it at the *Ledger* ... Bart Salisbury, the editors, and I ... you needed to extradite Farrow back here. Needed to get him away from the Kansas City authorities. Make him believe he was still partnering with you on the stolen jewels that were hiding in plain sight at Classic

Antiques ...."

Shorter was pulling out his cell phone and making a call.

"You calling Jarvis Pickens?" Franklin asked Shorter. "He's a corporate lawyer, isn't he? He handle criminal cases?"

"You're done here!" Weber snapped. "We've got nothing to say."

Both Weber and Shorter were glaring at him now.

Franklin rose slowly, then stood in front of the seated Shorter.

"Yeah," Franklin said casually. "Penny Shorter used those words: 'I've got nothing to say.' But then she did have something to say. And I escorted her willingly to the FBI. With her swollen cheek and black eye."

Franklin was glaring back at Shorter, who couldn't deal with it. He dropped his eyes. Then he dropped his arm holding the phone, and the phone fell to the mayor's luxurious carpet.

Franklin turned his head toward Weber.

"We'll be in touch, mayor. Thanks for your time."

Then Franklin walked from the noiseless room.

Back at the *Ledger*, he wrote a story draft covering his meeting with Penny Shorter, then with her brother and the mayor, including information about their flight to and from Kansas City, and their refusals to comment.

He emailed copies to Salsy and Ray Perry, suggesting that Salsy add whatever relevant information he might have garnered, and co-byline the article.

Then he thought of Betsy Jenkins, the *Ledger*'s revered business editor. He strode to her office, finding her tapping away at her keyboard. He gave a knock. Her head motioned him in. He slid to the chair by her desk.

"A visit from the *Ledger*'s answer to Batman," she drawled subtly, but smiling, her voice always as dry and smooth as the martinis she adored.

"How long you been at the *Ledger*, Betsy?"

"Since 1842, a year before you came on." She grabbed a gnawed chocolate bar off a napkin on her desk, gnawing a little more. "Why?"

"I've been gone a long time. Missed a lot. What can you tell me about Perry Shorter."

"Well, you're a veteran reporter. I figure you already know the basics, don't you?"

"The basics, yeah. His corporation. His connection to the mayor. His owning an antique store in the county."

"Antique store? I've never heard that come up in an interview or read it anywhere."

"Read my and Salsy's story tomorrow, and you'll see why. Ever hear of his involvement in anything underhanded?"

Betsy gnawed a little more and thought.

"No sir, I haven't. He grew up here. Been a combination of a corporate hustler and an ambitious community worker: chairman of Chamber drives, boards like Big Brothers and Second Start, the charity for convicts trying to get a new life in society."

"No stories of improprieties?"

"Not even rumors. What do you have on him?"

"Serious stuff." Franklin winked, rose, and moved to the door. "Betsy, please read the article tomorrow. And if you think of anything . . . ."

". . . I'll shine a spotlight on the clouds, and you can call me Commissioner."

She winked back. He laughed softly and left her.

Then he returned home to see if he might have received a message from Viper.

Back at the townhouse, opening the laptop, diving deep, an encrypted message awaited:

Taipan: Hoped to involve you in Operation Pressing Freedom. Have now moved on without you. Ready to implement. Trust you won't interfere. Semper Fi.

So . . . Ranch Hand had now evolved into a secret military operation: Pressing Freedom. One obviously not run by, but opposed to the federal government, if it involved killing the Attorney General. And it must reach beyond him. Viper would never just cut off a hand when he needed to eliminate an enemy. And he thought Franklin might interfere.

Franklin's mind was trying to match Viper's. He shut and replaced the laptop, moving quickly to his writing room and sitting at his computer. His writing-room windows framed the tops of oaks hinting at new leaves, and beyond the setting sun's darkening blue canvas with slivers of lavender clouds.

Viper's mind … the Constitution … eliminate the enemy ….

Sure. The Attorney General *was* the enemy. If Viper wanted him out of the way, he would also want to get rid of the fascist President who was running the show and appointed the Attorney General. But that would put the Vice President in charge of the country. He was a radical-right pseudo-Christian, considered by many press analyses to be even more dangerous than the President. Some analysts even had sneered that the President had chosen him because any foe of America would be terrified to assassinate the President and put the VP in the Oval Office.

So, if Viper is looking to assassinate the Big Three … who's next in line to succeed? And how would Viper react to that?

Franklin typed into Google: *U.S. presidential succession line.*

Links popped up. He clicked the first, which showed the legal line of successors:

President

Vice President

Speaker of the House

President pro tempore of the Senate

Secretary of State

Secretary of the Treasury

Secretary of Defense

Attorney General
Secretary of the Interior
Secretary of Agriculture
Secretary of Commerce
Secretary of Labor
Secretary of Health and Human Services
Secretary of Housing and Urban Development
Secretary of Transportation
Secretary of Energy
Secretary of Education
Secretary of Veterans Affairs
Secretary of Homeland Security

Franklin snuffed a gallows laugh, his mind leaping to Chubby Checker's voice and a spoken line from his '60s hit single "Limbo Rock," "How low can you go?"

"Franklin, you'll always be crazy," he whispered to himself.

His eyes focused on each federal office, analyzing each individual currently serving, judging how deep Viper might descend in his Pressing Freedom.

The House Speaker: ultra-conservative Midwesterner who wanted to eliminate programs for the poor and elderly, ranging from medical care to education. And excessively increasing tax breaks for the wealthy.

The Senate's President pro tempore: a near mirror of the House Speaker, only older and tougher.

Viper would hate both those political records.

Secretary of State: An emperor of Big Oil—former chief of the world's largest petroleum conglomerate. The President had clearly appointed him to assure America's control of Eurasian energy, and thus the effort to keep—in their minds—America as the world's lone superpower. And eliminate any U.S. move to oppose climate change. All the time hoping he could seal private business deals to make him and the prez richer.

Treasury Secretary: a soulless former Wall Street banker and also West Coast big-bank conglomerate CEO. He had screwed more clients, mortgage holders, and bank customers than the air held polluted molecules.

Viper would want to personally take such men out, even make them suffer first.

Who's next?

The Secretary of Defense. Bingo.

The Defense Secretary was a former highly decorated Marine general, retired. The conservative Senate had granted a special waiver so he could serve in the civilian secretary's position.

Franklin's memory began digging back. He and Viper had both met the future Secretary in '74 as the Vietnam War was closing down. The meeting was brief, in Da Nang, where all three were officers. The two secret assassins were preparing to move out on new separate missions. The third officer, a captain, had just arrived in 'Nam more for research, then to report back to the Pentagon.

Highly intellectual, carrying a copy of Marcus Aurelius's *Meditations* everywhere, the Pentagon researcher had earned the other two officers' immediate respect through his charisma and deep understanding of military history, evident in his conversation. He also showed them immediate respect:

"What are you two involved in now?" the Pentagon officer had asked.

Silence. Then Franklin:

"We're not really at liberty to say."

That was all it took. The intellectual then moved to questions about their hometowns, their plans after service, then smiled, shook hands, and left them. They would follow his career, up the ranks, into leadership positions all the way to General, and as head commander in the Middle East. Even had read about him after his retirement, his move to corporate boards and think tanks.

This guy, thought Franklin, Viper will not touch. This guy would be, in Viper's mind, at least a safe, if not good, President. One who respected the Constitution, and would follow it, including refusing to move into any foreign combat without Congressional approval.

So … why eliminate the Attorney General, who was next in the succession line *after* the Defense Secretary? Simply a buffer to help the new President? If so, how far down the list would Viper then want to move?

Franklin looked at the rest of the succession list.

Lightweights. Even idiots, a couple of them. No threat to the new President. Except for the Homeland Security Secretary, also a retired Marine Corps general. Would he be a Presidential cohort or foe in the new administration?

The two assassins also had brief encounters with him in 'Nam. He was a different brand than the current Defense Secretary: Not an intellectual, but bright. He had enlisted in the Marines after high school, not attending college until after 'Nam. Then worked hard, highly dedicated to the Marines, to those who served.

But what about those who didn't serve? Franklin had read about him as Homeland Security's chief. He questioned the former general's lack of concern for human rights. Would that continue under a new administration? Would the new President keep him on? Bring him closer as a counsel or confidant? Or push him out? Would Viper ask those questions?

The phone's ring interrupted Franklin's wondering. Cassie's voice sounded worried.

"I've been trying to call you. Did you not check your answering machine?"

"Oops. Sorry."

"When are you going to get a damn smartphone?"

"What's the matter?"

"I can't get in touch with Jessica. She's not at the office. She's not answering her phone. This whole thing with you and the police, the threats, has me rattled."

"Where do you think she might be? Where would she NOT answer her phone?"

"Ohhh, shit. Probably at Toby's. But I just don't know."

"Probably engaged in intimacy?"

"Yeah … probably …."

"… A little afternoon delight moving into evening?"

"Dammit, Reeves, that's not funny. I'm really worried."

"I'm sorry, babe. I understand. I'll go by and check."

"Oh … god … She'll hate me for that."

"She'll be miffed, but know you love her enough to find her. She'll get over."

As Franklin drove through the dusk, his mind stayed on Viper. Operation Pressing Freedom. If he was really planning erasing a limited hierarchy, it would take a team he knew and trusted intimately, people who'd been in contact with him a long time. He and Franklin were the only survivors of their 'Nam assassin days. So he obviously, through the years, must have developed new bonds.

Franklin pulled up at Toby's townhouse, some three miles from Franklin's abode. Jessica's car was parked behind his. No lights in the residence. But shyness wasn't on Franklin's resume.

He knocked on the door. Once decently. Then loud. Then louder. Finally the door opened. A mussed-haired Toby in a robe.

"What the hel … Oh … hi, Reeves."

"Sorry to bother you, Toby. This police thing I've been

involved in has Cassie spooked. Would you ask Jessica to please call her. Let her know she's with you. And ask her to be kind. It's just that her mother loves her deeply."

"Sure, I can do that. I hope everything's working out okay, with you and that police deal."

"So far so good. Man, I'm really sorry if I caused any coitus interruptus."

"Oh … we'll probably get refocused," Toby smiled.

Franklin smiled back, turned and left.

Franklin liked Toby. He respected Jessica, cared tenderly for her. And he could match her intellectually … a teacher of philosophy and history at the local university. An easy sense of humor and a black belt in karate. Renaissance man, Franklin thought, sniffing a grin.

Driving home, his mind went back to Viper.

Whatever Viper had planned in his operation, and however deep his kill list, the implementation would have to involve speed and coordination. Big time. More intricate with each life he wanted to take. Because each would be guarded, and on his own individual schedule, fulfilling his responsibilities of office.

Viper would have to possess an up-to-date itemization of each man's schedule. And he would have to erase each man on the same day, most likely within the same hour. Even faster. Because whenever one of those high-ranking officials was murdered … though Viper wouldn't consider it murder … he knew the others would automatically go into lockdown, with security moving them into the safest place possible. He would need to hit each target within a fifteen-minute framework, if not tighter.

Suddenly, Franklin was confronted by the peering eye through the beaded curtain. He couldn't push it away now. His psyche was too focused on the killing process. His body began shaking. He promptly pulled the car off the road and next to the curb, parking, dropping his skull back on the headrest, deep breathing, praying for the experience to be lifted from him. But the memory was persistent and forceful.

~

Da Nang. 1973. Young, virile, lonely, he was supposed to be finishing prep for moving out to a secret kill. But he was feeling feisty, rebellious, horny. He had left the air base and headed toward the city, just once taking advantage of his lone-wolf freedom to move off the base at will instead of under orders. Taking advantage of his superiors' trust. Dressed in civvies.

He maneuvered his way past the flooded rice fields into Da Nang's row of shanty bars and brothels, their cheap, slanted corrugated metal roofs altering reflections of the late day turning to dusk.

A bar. A brew. Then next door, grabbing a young beauty in her tattered silk desperate effort at elegance. Through the beaded curtain to the bed. Half an hour of tenderness and passion. Then softness and silence of lying together.

Then, it seemed, too much silence. A creak in the floor.

He turned to see an eye glaring through the curtain. Then a gun barrel slicing through the beads.

Franklin instantly was both rolling off the bed to his left and reflexively shoving the young woman to the right, out of firing range. But his hand slipped as he shoved. She stayed on the bed, startled.

Franklin was on the floor, the bed as partial cover from gunfire. His Glock now in his hand, blasting at the curtain. But the Vietcong gunman had riddled the bed with his machine gun's bullets, ripping through the prostitute's flesh and bone.

Then silence.

Cat-quick, Franklin was against the wall by the curtained entrance. He saw the gun on the floor, bloodied hands gripping it. Still. He kicked at the hands. Only a deadened response. He grabbed and ripped down the curtain, hurling it off to the side. The Vietcong killer's body laid motionless, blood seeping from two holes in the head, two in the neck, a half dozen in the chest. Blood now forming a distorted arc around the torso.

Franklin's eyes scanned the hall and room entrances for any movement. None. Only the sound of invisible women crying. He moved quickly to each room, three of the five occupied by half-nude women who had been rapidly deserted. He strode back to his room, jammed his foot angrily into the dead killer's back, and stepped to the bed. Beauty, gentleness, innocence corrupted by war, all gone now. Her earthen eyes were still open, mute horror distorting her mouth.

He was enraged. Swirling, he emptied his gun into the dead Vietcong. Grabbed and emptied the machine gun into him. Whirled and began slamming the rifle endlessly against the wall and floor until it finally began breaking apart. Threw the fragments through the hall. Then grabbed his combat knife, gouged out both the killer's eyes, scalped him viciously, stomped naked to the shanty's entrance and threw the scalp into the muddy street. Monsoon rains were growing heavy now, and the dark street was empty. Only peering, wary eyes in a few distant windows.

He returned to the room, used the bed sheet to wipe blood from his hands and arms, redressed, replaced a full clip into his pistol. He quickly fled through the rain, pausing only briefly in a deserted alley at a growing puddle to wash the remaining blood from his hands, face, and his knife. Then he was gone into the growing darkness.

Back at the base, he didn't stop to speak to anyone, unquestioned by the gate guards who knew him (but not his true mission), despite their being startled at his appearance, later mumbling to each other he must have won a bar fight. Went to his small, private tent, stripped and redressed into military wear. He grabbed and downed a beer. Then he made his way to a prepped Huey Slick, its props already whirling and ready. He provided directions. It rose and disappeared into the hard rain of night.

~

Franklin had tilted his Toyota seat's back as far as possible, lay at that slanted angle, trying to push his body out of sight from the car windows, sobbing uncontrollably.

He didn't know how long it took. But the crying ceased. His heavy sobbing turned to deep breathing, a weak attempt at meditation. His whispered prayers seemed empty.

Eventually his mind crawled back to the present. He began thinking of Evelyn, missing her. Missing Cassie. Missing Jessica. Missing Melissa. Missing Laura. Missing Heather. Missing them all and their collective warm smiles and hearts. A different crying now. A sense of hope.

He tilted his car seat back up. Sat for a long moment. Then started the Toyota and pulled it back onto the now-dark street.

His body was soaked with sweat. He felt filthy ... the grime and sin of war grafted to him. He craved spiritual peace and security. He needed to make his way to the Grace Place. And he did.

After the meeting, a sponsee approached him cautiously, asked if he was all right. Franklin quickly put the attention back on the young man. He suggested they meet the next day and review a Step. The sponsee agreed.

Franklin turned to walk away. His sponsor stood there, gazing at him. Together, they walked out to Franklin's car and stopped, staring at each other.

"You look like shit. Are you alright?" the sponsor

asked, scratching his gray curly hair.

"Old war traumas coming back. Happens rarely, but more often than I care for."

"You want to sit and talk a little?"

"For a bit, yeah. Thanks."

They talked for a bit, not wasting words. Franklin wasn't specific. Just told him the violent past refuses to leave, like their alcoholic disease. Always lurking.

Back at the townhouse, he opened the door and stood in the living room's blackness, the space seeming an endless void. Then his eyes grew accustomed to the hints of light through the closed-blind windows, and shadowy outlines of furniture.

He whispered to the listening universe.

"Thank you for keeping me sober. Thank you for all."

And he meant *all*. Every experience. Every bit of environment. Every intricate molecule that formed him and his life. Visions ran through him of dangerous instances, moments so close to finality, seconds which swept past, tilted just a certain way, allowing him to stand here now in what was, in reality, his space. His comfortable space. He thought of Robert Penn Warren, *A Place to Come To.*

He closed and locked the door. Didn't bother to turn on a light. Stepped to and fell into his favorite chair. Leaned back, heeled off his shoes, and closed his eyes, deep breathing into an involuntary sleep.

His eyes were slowly opening now. Still dark.

Semi-sleep. His psyche slowly rising. Time to write.

At his keyboard, his fingers seemed to move independent of his body. Before long, a draft:

Night Prayer

Overwhelm us with your light energy,
your heat of serenity and passion,
your dear separations and synergy
of near planets and stars, comets and moons
composing our galaxy and every
universe. Show us how you make up all
and our place within your all. You carry
existence like a lighted candle, call
for our honest actions of faith and love
through simple caresses and softest words.
If you must, brandish your tight-fisted glove
to save us, crushing weapons and absurd
machines of fear. If you must, hurl and crack
the whip, sing to us, but keep us on track.

~

Franklin saved the writing in a file. Printed out a hard copy and laid it on the keyboard to look at later. Then he rose and headed to his bed.

After the early-morning workout, he sat over breakfast with the sponsee. They spoke of the Second step, of being restored to sanity. Franklin repeated the mantra: "One day at a time. We live one day at a time. We work on growing conscious contact with the higher power one day at a time. We can't restore ourselves to sanity. We seek the higher power's restoration. One day at a time."

"I'm saying this not only for you, but to also remind me," Franklin said. The sponsee understood.

10

A CUCKOO CLOCK

Two days had passed. The town's politicos were abuzz and taken aback with the *Ledger* story, co-bylined by Franklin and Salsy, connecting the mayor and his crony with a scandal involving jewel theft, fencing, and murder.

Franklin still refused to return any phone calls from the media, as did Salsy. Confronted in person a couple of times while having lunch, they echoed, "Read our take in the *Ledger*."

But now it was March 13 … four days from Viper's activating Operation Pressing Freedom. Franklin had to do something. But what? He couldn't go to the authorities. His vow to secrecy remained. In fact, with no hint on his old military record of his true activities, who would believe him?

"The prosecutor would like to talk to you."

Franklin looked up from his desk at a frowning Ray

Perry.

"What do you recommend?" Franklin asked.

Perry stared at him, then looked up and out at nothing, then back at Franklin.

"Fuck him. Go to his office. Talk to him. Then write a story about it."

Franklin made a call to Connie Storyk, the *Ledger's* courthouse reporter. Then he left for the county offices.

A handsome hunk in his mid-forties, Garrison Field was prosecutor of the state's largest county. Ambitious. Craving good press on his aggressiveness. Lusting to be governor. Franklin sat calmly in the lawyer's mahogany office, the politician eyeing him closely.

"I'm curious," drawled Field, wearing a smirk, obviously sold on his own savvy. "You've done really good work on those stories of yours."

Franklin didn't respond. Sat quietly, thinking to himself, okay, so he's going to give me the one-man good cop-bad cop routine.

"I'm wondering how you got clued into this alleged conspiracy. You've taken a straightforward police report on shooting a robber and turned it into a major political scandal."

"Got a phone call when I was at the paper. An anonymous witness of the shooting. His statements proved true. Then the two rogue cops roughing Salsy and me up. I didn't go looking for either of those experiences. They found me."

"And I'm very curious how you disarmed those two undercover cops."

Franklin repeated his line: He works out a lot. Knows some karate. Since he's an old guy, it must have caught the two thugs by surprise.

"And how did you stumble onto the little antiques store in the county, connect that to all this?"

"A cuckoo clock."

"What?"

"One of the *Ledger* reporters had told me about buying a clock at Classic Antiques. When I was traveling the county, conducting interviews on the proposed annexation, I passed the antiques store, remembered the clock, and decided to go in and get another interview. Saw an impressive jewelry collection. Penny Shorter told me her name, and the name of the owner, her brother."

"That's it?"

"That's it. Then with Salsy's information, just started connecting dots."

Silence.

"You have anything against Mr. Shorter or the mayor? Any reason to draw them into this thing?"

That was the last question. Franklin's patience was waning. He turned it.

"What information do you have on the rogue cops?" he asked the prosecutor.

"What?"

"Why haven't you found the killers? You've got a stable of investigators. You haven't even issued a report of your efforts to track them down. Why not?"

"You got a lot of gall, Franklin. Questioning me after I've ordered you in here."

"You didn't order me in here … Field. If you had tried to order me in here, I wouldn't have come, and the *Ledger* would have backed me. I responded to your suggestion to come, so I could get a story."

"A stor …."

Franklin didn't allow him time for another echo.

"I had a little talk with Connie Storyk, the *Ledger*'s county reporter. Found out some interesting facts about you."

"Wha …."

"Seems Perry Shorter was also a major financial backer of *your* campaign. Seems you're an old buddy of the mayor. Seems you got his quiet support in your race for prosecutor. Seems you all meet regularly at night … at old Milt Rayburn's pharmacy … old Milt Rayburn the former mayor and political boss … to calculate how to make you governor. Seems you've already started a war chest."

"Now you wait a min …."

"Seems you're in a quandary. You've got a murder case tossed in your lap involving the mayor, the police, and a rich business guy which, if you won the case, would assure your chances for governor. But if you follow through, you're dissolving your political and financial support."

Field had grown beet-red, was breathing heavily, but was clearly shocked now into silence.

"And, if you follow through, it might turn out you're somehow connected to this fence operation."

Field shot up from his chair, leaning forward on his desk, then starting to move around it. Franklin sat cool and still, feeling the power.

"I wouldn't," Franklin said, his voice so coldly calm it caused Field to stop. "It wouldn't look good in my story tomorrow about our interview."

Field plopped back in his big leather chair, limp now.

"So … you have any comment about how the investigation's progressing? The location of the rogue cops?"

Field sat silent, eyes blazing.

"Any comment about Penny Shorter going to the FBI? Have you heard from the FBI?"

Silence. Blazing.

"No? Well … I guess this interview's over. Thanks for your time, Mr. Prosecutor."

Franklin rose and walked out of the deadened stillness.

Back at the *Ledger*, he wrote the story carefully, emphasizing the known information about Field's connection to Weber and Shorter, the businessman's funding his campaign, and the meetings at the pharmacy. He noted that Field had no comment about any of it. Story complete, he filed it, giving Connie Storyk a co-byline with him. Then emailed a copy to her.

Seated at the Caboose with the crew, Franklin sipped on his seltzer and lime, his mind not on Field or the murder, but on Operation Pressing Freedom.

"Reeves … Reeves, my man." The stoned Will Hollis echoed his usual hollow benevolence. Franklin watched him, forced a smile and nodded, not speaking.

"You're a quiet one this evening, Mr. Franklin," the semi-concerned Salsy slurred. "This swelling scandal not gettin' to you, is it?"

Franklin turned and studied Salsy. He needed to make a decision. And he did.

"Salsy, can I talk to you outside?"

"Sure. Let's wander."

The March air still hinted at chill, the passing cars' lights beginning to ignite as the sun escaped the horizon. Franklin gazed out beyond the parking lot, actually planning the rest of the night and tomorrow. Salsy waited.

"Salsy, I'm going to leave this cop murder caper with you. I need to go out of town for a few days."

"Oka-a-ay," Salsy said, his elongated response more a question.

"Tell Perry I couldn't avoid it. It's a responsibility I have to attend to."

"Oka-a-ay …."

Franklin turned and looked at Salsy, then did something he never did with his fellow reporters. He reached out and shook his hand.

"You've done a helluva job on this murder case."

"You more," Salsy responded.

Then Franklin left him.

⁓

Franklin knocked twice on the door, and Georgia Matthews opened it. Surprised to see him, she smiled, looking to both sides of him.

"Hi, Reeves! Is … Cassie … not with you?"

"No, Georgia. Is the Senator in? I need to talk with him."

"Sure, c'mon in. He's in the den reading."

In the den, the Senator looked up from his book and seeing Franklin, began rising to his feet.

"Don't get up, Senator."

"I always rise to express due respect," he said, smiling.

Franklin smiled and shook his hand.

"I'm sorry to bother you, but it's important."

"Cassie's not with you?"

"No."

Carson Mathews motioned Franklin to the near love seat, and returned to his chair. He studied his visitor closely.

"How can I help you, Reeves?"

"Two things. First, I need to take a private plane to New York. Soon as possible. Anybody owe you a favor?"

"I know a couple of people. Can you tell me what this is about?"

"I wish I could … but no."

"Okay. What's the second thing?"

"It won't matter if I can't do this first thing."

The Senator studied him. Then he decided to act, more because of Franklin's connection to Cassie, who Mathews owed so much. But also because he admired Franklin, and trusted him.

Mathews reached to the small table next to his chair, taking his smartphone. He flipped through his directory, making a call, but unable to make contact. He made a second call.

"Ben, I need a big favor. A cohort needs a plane to New York, tonight if possible. You will? Two hours? Okay. Ben, I really appreciate this. His name is Reeves Franklin … yes, the reporter who wrote about the mayor and Shorter. But I think this trip is about something else."

The Senator looked at Franklin to concur, and his visitor nodded yes.

"This is a completely different matter. Okay. Ben, if there's ever anything I can do for you … I know … I know I have. Okay. Let's say we're even. Let's lunch next week and celebrate our long friendship. I'm footing it. Good … thanks … Bye."

"Thank you, Senator."

"You're welcome. What's number two?"

"Strictly between you and me … not even Georgia … please."

"Sure."

"If something happens … and I don't come back … I'm going to ask you to be there for Cassie."

Mathews focused more heavily on his visitor, obviously wishing to know more, but honoring the confidence.

"Okay. Reeves, I know a lot of people, including in New York. If there's anything I can do …"

"I wish there was. There's not. This involves an oath … and a vow … and I need to do what I can to make things end well."

Mathews breathed out long.

"Wow," he sighed oh so softly. "I wish I could help."

"You've helped greatly by granting my two requests."

"I spoke with Ben Harkland, a very old friend. His pilot, Mike Farris, will be at Barrett Air Service waiting. In two hours, he'll be ready to take you."

Franklin rose, thanked the Senator, and left him and his wife at their front door, wishing him well.

On his way to Cassie's, he stopped off at Kroger's, searched and made a purchase, then on to her house.

She opened the door, surprised and happily hugging him. He hugged her back, tightly, alerting her.

"Reeves … what is it?"

Their caress calmed him. He smiled at her.

"I'm flying to New York tonight. Should be back in a couple of days."

"What is it?"

"A possible story … maybe even a book idea … but I don't want to jinx it by talking about it."

She winced at him suspiciously.

"Okay, Franklin … you're gonna meet a stripper, aren't you? Run off to Canada."

"Man … you can read me like a porn novel … hot and heavy."

She laughed, hugged him again. Studied him, but decided not to question his intent any further.

"Can I drive you to the airport?"

"No. Ol' Toyota's whinnying and ready to ride. Wish me luck."

"Good luck."

"In fact … pray for me … okay?"

"Reeves? Will you call? Let me know you got there okay?"

He reached in his pocket, pulled out a TracFone and wiggled it in front of her.

"An LG Treasure LTE … whatever that means," he said, smiling. "Guaranteed to be able to reach you from Manhattan."

"Yeah. Manhattan, Kansas?"

He faked a laugh, then grabbed, hugged her long, kissed her longer. Then:

"See ya," he said softly.

"See ya."

And he was in the car, on the road to his townhouse.

In his bedroom, he tossed a couple day's clothes into a backpack, retrieved his Glock and combat knife—the reason he needed a private flight and not a public airline with the TSA and X-ray machines. Also, if the crafty Viper was monitoring him, he'd realize he was coming if he flew on an airline. He wrapped his weapons in a sweatshirt, stuffed them deep in the pack. He judged the amount of cash he would need, walleted it, and headed out.

11

A SLIGHT TREMOR

FRANKLIN FELT BOTH SPECIAL AND LONELY, the only passenger in the Cessna CJ2, built to seat nine. Even sitting at the front right window, to him the pilot Mike Farris seemed far away. He had told Franklin the flight time would be about four hours to LaGuardia, slowed some by predicted heavy turbulence over Washington, D.C.

"Isn't there always heavy turbulence over Washington?" Franklin had quipped.

Farris had responded with a genuine laugh, adding, "Yeah, and we're paying for it."

"More ways than one."

Another laugh, and then to the cockpit.

It was closing in on 10:00 pm, and Franklin decided to shut his eyes, deep breathe, offer some prayers, feeling that would relax him into sleep. But he began to grow more intense, rhythms began rising, and he turned to look out at the distant lights signaling the state's rural towns. He grabbed his backpack, pulled from it a small notebook and ballpoint pen, opened to a fresh page, and began to write.

Eventually he had drafted a sonnet:

THIS NIGHT

This night of our aesthetic agony,
this atmosphere which dissolves our breathing,
this distorting blackness and light we see
pouring through us with hypnotic seething
of dying stars, can we conceive its soul
somehow in our poems, in our sculptures
molded with course sands, raw silks slashed yet whole
at once—image of real lives ruptured
beyond repair yet healing through soft touch?
Can we still stand and hear our human songs—
simple lyrics like *I love you so much*?
Can we still caress and dance all night long
to passion's music deep within us, our
eyes igniting all galaxies' power?

~

He read the results over a couple of times. Thanked the Muse, as always, for every gift, for this gift.

He was suddenly tired and relaxed. He closed his eyes, the jet engines' wheezing hum offering a breathing mantra.

He woke to Mike Farris lightly tapping his shoulder, his soft voice announcing, "Mr. Franklin … we're here, sir."

"Mmm … What time is it?"

"2:20 a.m. New York time."

"Mmm … Just over three hours. I miss the Washington turbulence?"

"We got lucky. Congress was in recess."

~

Now the early morning of March 14. Franklin told the pilot he could return at will without him. He'd be in New York at least three days. They shook hands, and Franklin headed into LaGuardia's terminal to make his way to a cab.

Franklin had called the Washington Square Hotel from Far River, was lucky to get a just-vacated room. He had always liked visiting folks at the quaint Waverly Place locale. It was 4:10 a.m. when he plopped down on the corner of one twin bed in the small, calming room with cream-colored walls. He gazed sleepily at the trio of portraits above the bed's headboard: three different, luscious head shots of a young Liz Taylor, each dark frame decorated in its bottom left corner with a pair of painted violet roses.

He needed to sleep some more. Then, refreshed by rest and a good breakfast, he would begin his search to find Fitz, knowing that by now—five years since their last meeting—he had changed residences four or five times.

Up just after 9:00, Franklin shaved, showered, went to a nearby Greek deli for an omelet, sausage, and wheat toast, opting for iced tea which applied less stomach stress than coffee. Then he went back to his room, pulled out his new wireless phone, and called Cassie. They talked softly and warmly, like sweet cocoa coating the tongue. He couldn't tell her how he cherished each word. How he didn't know what the future held. After they spoke, he sat and prayed.

~

Outside, he was grateful for the sunny morning. It warmed the Manhattan March air's lingering cold. He walked around the New York University area and Washington Square Park. Eventually he found himself at the New York Sports Club on Mercer. He went in and approached the muscleman behind the counter.

"I'm looking for a gym with a broad range of weights, a pool, and heavy bag for hand and foot combat exercises," Franklin told him.

The young mammoth flexed his arms and lips unconsciously, thinking. He knew of only three, the closest on Washington Street.

Franklin headed west, pleased to be walking again in the Manhattan chill. Eventually he reached his destination, headed inside to converse with another behemoth.

"I'm back in the city after three years; looking for an old buddy," Franklin offered. "Wondering if he works out here."

"What's his name?"

"That's a good question. He's had a few ex-wives sending private dicks to try and find him, so he's been known to change his name."

"You're kinda old to be a detective, aren't ya?"

"Too old to be much of anything," Franklin smiled.

"Naw, I'm an ancient reporter, one of the lost generation that finally retired from the *Greenwich Gazette*. We've been buddies since the '60s. In the military together. He's an Irish-American New Yorker pushing seventy, but doesn't look it. Probably in better shape than any of the young studs you have saunter through here, though you wouldn't expect it from looking at him. He likes the treadmill, bike, weights, swimming, and is avid about the heavy bag for hand and foot combat exercises."

"Yeah. He used to work out here regularly. Man, he could wear you out just watching him. Haven't seen him for nearly a year."

"You have a similar gym somewhere in town? A guy at the Sports Club said he knew of only two others with the heavy bag and other offerings I mentioned."

"Yeah, I think that's all I'm aware of. You might try Power Gym on Canal Street. They've got all the goods."

It was an older gym, the kind Franklin felt Fitz would relish, with the warm, stale smell of old sweat from the moment you walked into the exercise room. Smaller and more comfortable than the more modern franchises. The manager, a graying, suspicious native New Yorker, wouldn't admit if he had a customer meeting Fitz's description, but let Franklin look around.

"You open 24/7?" Franklin queried.

"Almost. Open at 5:00 a.m. everyday. Close at eleven."

5:00 a.m. would work for Fitz. Franklin thanked the

man, and decided, without revealing it, that he'd check back the next early morning. If that didn't work, he'd take a cab up to the third similar gym in the East '70s, though that location seemed too uppity for Fitz.

Franklin found himself sitting in Washington Square Park, basking in near-noon sunlight, reading the *Times,* like the old days. Then he sauntered over to the Quantum Leap on Thompson Street, not far from his old studio. He was pleased to see his favorite waitress, Doree, still surviving, splitting time between patiently serving customers and her passion for ballet with a small Village company. She had always loved giving Franklin a warm, elongated hug, that he loved returning; and they repeated the ritual when she spied him coming in the door.

Munching on shrimp and salmon tacos with brown rice, he decided to thumb through the latest issue of *Time Out*, see if he might site a low-key folk performance to attend later. His eyes scanned the listings … and suddenly stopped. Warmth surged through his body.

Heather would be playing and singing at 8:00 p.m. at the Nearhere Café. Her smiling eyes glowed in the photo. He probably shouldn't go … but he would.

By 6:00 p.m., he was at one of his old regular meetings in Soho. A crowd of just over seventy went through the ritual of pre-meeting chatter, then stillness as a speaker shared his experience, strength and hope.

After the hour gathering, he was walking out when

a man's voice softly called, "Reeves?" Franklin recognized him as a former sponsee, still keeping his top priority. They agreed to a quick burger.

By 7:45, Franklin had made his way to the Nearhere Café, slipping into the last front-row seat, gratefully at the row's right end, in case he decided to make a quick exit if the feelings began clawing at him. He glanced around, recalling the East Village institution's warmth with its barn-wood paneling and hanging metal lamps.

At eight on the dot, Heather appeared, her sunrise hair flowing past her shoulders, caressing the full but not-emphasized breasts under her navy-blue, long-sleeve dress that stretched loosely past her waist to her dark slippers. She didn't look out at her audience, now grown to just over one hundred, but strapped on and tuned her cream-wood six-string guitar.

She had organized a new small band a few years ago, but this night had chosen to play solo. Tilting her mike, wincing a bit at first from the stage lights, she soon adjusted, and opened with a soft ballad, one of her many original songs from the gut, with fresh lyrics and rhythms designed to catch the listener off-guard. And they did, the audience growing silent, concentrating on her blending of vocals and fretwork. Franklin would watch her, then slowly turn to view the brief portion of the crowd visible to him. Then focus back on her sacred face caught in spotlight, and soft soprano with a magnetic hint of rasp, a voice to break hearts even if one hadn't intimately held her, as Franklin had.

After a handful of originals, she seemed more relaxed by the consistent warm applause. Then, with a couple of friendly called requests from the audience for her older creations, she smiled, and began looking out at her faithful.

She was scanning the crowd from her right to left. Then she reached the front row's end, and her eyes met Franklin's. Her smile faded quickly to just a touch of open mouth. Franklin knew that look, a facial expression of curiosity which actually masked shock. Then she began to smile again, but a different smile, the one he often would see when they would search and find each other on the street after work, meeting for dinner and a night together.

She began to strum the guitar, her clear-river eyes staying on him, her smile now soft and sure. He recognized the easy tune, its deceptive tenderness setting up the ear for the surprise of understated but passionate lyrics. A song she had written for him, about him and them—the struggle, the sweetness, the questioning of pleasure and pain.

How could they both not see each other's tears forming as she moved to the ballad's subtle yet wrenching end, leaving the listener with the ultimate question. Then silence. It seemed the mute house had emptied. Then applause rose like an ocean swell.

"Let's break for fifteen minutes," she said softly into the mike. "I'll see ya soon."

Applause and people rising, most staying at their seats,

simply stretching and conversing. She moved across the small stage toward Franklin, and he rose, stepping toward her. She bent to her haunches and gazed down at him.

"Hi," she almost whispered.

"Hi."

"What are you doing here? I thought you'd left New York."

"Now, how would you know that?"

She grimaced slightly, as if nicked by insult.

"You here with anybody?" she asked.

"Just the Muse. I was out wandering, and She nudged me this way."

"I'll sing about another half hour after the break. Then turn it over to the next act."

She tilted her head, as if trying to read his availability.

"Could we talk after? Maybe get a coffee?"

"Yes."

She didn't smile, but her face grew rose-warm. She reached down and touched his shoulder. Then she stood and trotted back behind the makeshift curtain.

Later, they lounged at a coffee house a block from the Nearhere. A lone young man played a solo guitar, not singing, simply covering old standards, but with a lovely individual interpretation.

They sat in a far corner, where the music and small crowd wouldn't disturb them. Spoke softly of old acquaintances, laughed at their private jokes. Then grew quiet.

"How's your family?" Franklin finally asked.

"Good. Jeff's keeping the two boys so I can perform."

"What are their names?"

"Dylan and Thomas."

"You're kidding?"

She laughed gently, shyly, responding, "You know me and poetry."

"And he let you get away with that?"

She laughed louder, then caught herself. Smiled and shrugged.

"How are you, Heather?"

She looked off into space, then over toward the guitarist. Thought for a moment, then turned and gazed straight at him.

"I probably shouldn't have left," she said with a slight tremor.

"You probably should have. I wanted to be good for you, but I don't think I was. We both still had a lot to work through … to discover."

"We were good for each other … and we weren't … I wanted to give myself to you … but …."

Silence.

"I know," he nearly whispered.

She sighed, rose slowly, took hold of her navy-blue wool jacket on the chair's back. He stood and helped her put it on. She picked up her guitar case. They stood and looked through each other. She leaned forward, kissed his mouth ever so softly. Stepped back. Raised her right hand, her fingers gently touching his lips. Then she turned and hurriedly walked away, through the front door, down the sidewalk, and out of sight.

Franklin wanted to go after her. But he didn't. He sat, studied her empty coffee cup, finished his peppermint tea, paid the bill and left. Checking his watch, he saw 10:46. He had time to make the 11:00 p.m. meeting at his old home group. And he did.

After that, falling into bed, he set the clock alarm for 4:30 a.m. He closed his eyes and prayed.

12

ENDGAME

THE ALARM WAS JUST OBNOXIOUS ENOUGH. No way to ignore it. He breathed out. Remembered what was important: "On awaking, we ask You to direct our thinking. Our feelings. Our words. Our actions." He asked guidance in practicing the Steps in all affairs.

After the shower and dressing, he called Evelyn on his new phone. He knew his daughter would probably still be asleep. But if he didn't call now, he might not have another chance. He got her voicemail.

"Hello, my dear daughter. I'm in New York. Have an assignment I need to complete. Thinking of you and wanted to call while I can. Sorry it's so early. I love you."

He suddenly began choking on the last sentence, his mind shoving him with the idea that he might never speak to her again. He clicked the phone off, donned his jacket, cap and backpack, and headed out the door. Grabbed a quick bite at the same Greek deli.

Thought to himself, March 15. He now had only two days—today and tomorrow—to find Fitz, talk him out of his March 17 assassinations.

He reached the Canal Street gym at 5:47. Walking in, he looked at the sleepy-eyed manager. The man stared at him, as if questioning what to do. Then he gave a what-the-hell shrug, and nodded toward the exercise room. Franklin went there.

Fitz was on the heavy bag, his lethal hands and feet appearing nearly as quick as when in their prime. Franklin kept his distance, watching in silence. He admired his old Corps mate's maneuvers, was swept briefly back to those ancient days of combat training, then back to the reality: Fitz was determined to implement Operation Pressing Freedom. To alter history. Could Franklin convince him not to? What would Franklin do if he couldn't?

He knew Fitz's alert senses had caught sight of him as soon as he had entered. So he waited until the kicking warrior decided to take a break. Finally he did, breathing heavily, walking and grabbing his towel off a near weight rack, and turning, staring at Franklin, the slightest smile curling his lips.

Franklin walked to him, stopped within arms distance, the two old comrades staring calmly at each other.

"I thought we weren't ever gonna do this again," Fitz

said almost lightly.

"Thought it was a good time to come visit," Franklin responded with a slight smile.

"Figured you would. I'll get a shower. Then we can head to my place and talk."

Franklin nodded, and Fitz went to the locker room.

A windy mist as Franklin found himself again on Washington Street. They didn't speak of the present, knowing they'd save that for their time in private.

"You remember how often we had to maneuver in weather like this," Fitz asked.

"Not really," Franklin responded, studying the gray sky. "I mostly remember the heavy rains. Wondering if I'd survive them, much less the danger of the job."

"Rain rain rain," Fitz almost mumbled. "Seemed like we were always getting soaked. Guess we were the cleanest killers in Southeast Asia."

"And then being pushed into that Middle East furnace. How could you not want to kill in weather like that?"

Fitz laughed. Franklin didn't.

They were in the 600 block of Washington now.

"This is a part of the Village's Historic District extension," Fitz commented. "Once I turned seventy, I decided to get a little class. Live quiet but cool."

He stopped at a federal-style townhouse, opened the side gate. Franklin followed him back to a two-story carriage house, where Fitz stepped to its white windowed door, and pulled out a key. Inside they walked through a narrow living room with old wood floor and fireplace, leading to a basic, bare kitchen. Both rooms lacked furniture.

"You're kidding," Franklin said, his eyes glancing around the empty space.

"All the comforts of home," Fitz said with a smirk.

"You just move in?"

"You know better."

He followed Fitz up the tight old stairway to the second floor. Two more small rooms, one empty, the second with a cot up against the wall. In the center, a school lunch-room-style table with two metal chairs, one across from the other on each of the table's long sides. On the tabletop, three laptops lay shut next to each other.

"You still like peppermint tea?" Fitz asked.

"Had some last night. Warms the tummy."

"Be right back. Make yourself comfortable at the king's table."

He moved out of the room and down the stairs. Franklin took off his backpack, set it by the cot, removed his jacket and cap, and sat at the table, looking at but not touching the three laptops. Then he scanned the room, the two windows, smudged but letting in light. The cot covered with a single blanket and thin pillow.

Soon he heard the water kettle whistling downstairs. In a couple of minutes, Fitz walked in with two steaming cups. He put one in front of Franklin, the tea bag's string and label dangling from the brim.

"It's not Twinings," Fitz revealed. "Bigelow. Sorry."

"Bigelow's welcome."

Fitz blew on his tea, then took a couple of sips. Leaned back in his chair, put his hands behind his head, and stared at Franklin.

His guest sipped his tea, welcomed the warmth, the healthy taste of it. Thought a second about sipping it last night with Heather. Pushed that back, and stared back at his host.

Fitz broke a long silence:

"So …" and he waited.

"So, thought I'd come to New York. See if I could talk Viper out of implementing Operation Pressing Freedom."

"Viper's not available."

"Not sure his operation's constitutional. You know our oath."

"Yeah, you and I know our oath. But you don't know what the operation consists of."

"I know it involves cleaning the Attorney General. That's what you wanted me to do on March 17."

"That's been scrapped."

"Pressing Freedom?"

"No. Just the AG. March 17 is out. And he's a lightweight, too much trouble for today."

"Today?"

"Yeah. Today. March 15. The Ides of March. Ironic,

huh?"

"You mean …"

"Yeah. Caesar changed his plans. So everything had to shift. He had been scheduled for New York on the seventeenth. Moved it up to today. To coincide with the Czar's decision to visit him at the palace."

Fitz took a long draw of his tea, smiling at his guest. Franklin sat thinking, also taking a couple of gulps, warmth coating his throat.

"You mean the Russian president's coming to New York? There was nothing in yesterday's *Times*."

"No. White House kept it secret. Released it last night while you were enjoying music and meeting the old love."

Franklin smiled.

"Yeah," said Fitz. "I knew you'd come. The invitation to kill. Then the note asking you to stay out. Too tempting."

"I didn't come to kill. I came to talk Viper out of killing."

"Won't happen. Where are your weapons?"

"In my backpack." Franklin took a big swig of tea, his habit of finishing a cup before it cooled. "I didn't bring the weapons for you. But I wasn't sure how things would unfold. If someone I didn't know might be after us."

"Glock and knife?"

"My favorites."

"Mine too."

They watched each other. Franklin finished his tea,

and Fitz took a long drink of his.

"You want another?" Fitz asked.

"No. I'm all right."

Fitz sat there, silently watching him.

"The AG's out," said Franklin. "How deep are you going down the succession list? Stop at the Defense Secretary?"

"Why?"

"You know why. The Constitution's the deal here. And I know you. We met him once, and have watched the guy. You believe he'll follow the Constitution while the others won't."

Fitz stared, smiling.

"How in hell do you even think you can maneuver against all the intelligence and security that protects the President and VP alone?" Franklin asked.

Fitz leaned forward, staring at Franklin.

"How has Caesar treated the intelligence community? National security?"

Franklin winced, beginning to see. "With contempt. He's complained about their capabilities … even refused to receive some of their reports."

"You know what that means," Fitz smiled. "It means more than just insulting them. To them, he's questioning their patriotism. And now they see him challenging the Constitution. Freedom of the press. Freedom of expression. He's denying climate change. Moving us closer to nuclear war. More."

Suddenly Franklin was feeling tired. The travel? The lack of sleep last night?

"Intelligence and security will *allow* us in," Fitz declared, his voice emphasizing permission. "They'll blame our attack on radical Islamic terrorists. Admit publicly their fumbling the ball. Take the political and public hits. Then be ready to tightly guard the new leadership and see their own roles renewed and respected again. They'll even lose some of their faithful in our attack. Necessary for appearances, and for the greater good."

Franklin was starting to feel warm. Not tea warm. Stress warm. He was sweating. This wasn't like him. His lips and tongue felt as if they were being jabbed by pins. He was weakening, his head beginning to throb. His arms and legs growing numb. He suddenly glared at Fitz.

"Y … you … f … fuck …."

Fitz shrugged his shoulders matter-of-factly.

Franklin fell forward, though he didn't feel it, his head and shoulders slamming onto the table. His body beginning to slide from the chair.

Fitz rose and walked around to him. He grabbed Franklin under his arms, lifted him and placed him on the cot, sitting him up facing the table, placing the thin pillow behind his head.

"I couldn't take the chance on you messing this up," Fitz said calmly, stretching Franklin's legs out, as if trying to make him comfortable.

Fitz walked over to the closet. Pulled out a portable respirator box and brought it to the cot. Unpacking the respirator, he placed the plastic tubes in Franklin's nostrils, attaching a strap around his head to secure the tubes, then plugged the other tube ends into the machine, turning it on. Franklin could hear but not feel the flow of air.

"You know I don't want to hurt or kill you," Fitz said. "You're not the enemy. You're a value to this nation."

He moved to the table, grabbed a chair, put it by the cot and sat down, looking at Franklin.

"You're gonna be paralyzed but conscious for a while," Fitz advised. "I measured out a proper amount of TZ … saxitoxin. The major problem could be respiratory failure. So we're countering that with the respirator. It's solid. I've tested it myself."

Fitz turned the chair around to the table, opened each of the laptops, and began diving deep to the Dark Web on each one.

Franklin remained conscious but helpless. His eyes and hearing were clear. He seemed to be breathing fine. But his body lay numb and limp.

His eyes were able to follow Fitz as he moved to and fro among the laptops. He could clearly see each screen, the traveling through the Dark Web on each. Then video pictures of locations began appearing on each, live. Fitz began clicking on one screen, calling up four separate locations. Then four on the second laptop. Then four on the third. All appearing to be separate places.

Once Fitz seemed satisfied he was in visual contact with each site, he turned the chair and faced Franklin.

"You know the deal," Fitz said to him. "These guys are fascists. Whether they plan to or not, they'll bring this nation down. And they've already started with their unconstitutional actions. They are the enemy."

He studied Franklin, who was able to move his eyes but nothing else. He stared at Fitz.

"We've been planning this for over a year. When we saw the possibility that Caesar might get in the White House. I've got some good guys … twelve of 'em … The Apostles."

Fitz smiled at Franklin, letting him absorb the lethal irony.

"They're old vets like us, from every military branch. All involved in espionage. Silent and secret. Attack alone and by surprise. Get in fast and out fast. Just like we would. All decades away from active service and any notice by almost all the intelligence community. Calculatingly ignored by its chiefs.

"I got a weapons supplier, a hefty arsenal, divided it among The Apostles, appropriate to each location's challenge. Unfortunately, I had to erase the weapons guy to assure his silence. But Washington understands collateral damage, don't they?"

He smiled again. Gave Franklin a pat on the leg.

"We're all systems go starting …" Fitz checked his

watch, then the digital clocks on each screen. They read 9:44 am, March 15. "… in sixteen minutes. Every Apostle must have cleaned his target as soon after 10:00 a.m. as possible, certainly no later than 10:10, since each target would be covered and secured by then, once they heard an attack was on. But you know all this, don't you?"

He smiled and patted Franklin's leg again.

"Here's who's going down, in order from least to most importance … like they'd do on the *Tonight Show* …."

Fitz gave a snicker, shook his head at his morbid humor. Then sat and watched Franklin, making sure he was still conscious and staring, and that his breathing was normal.

Then Fitz turned to the laptop on the far left. He switched to a live video of a suburban block. With each picture switch, he described the coming victims to Franklin.

"Number twelve: the House Speaker. He's at his D.C. home this morning in Maryland. He's third in succession but a lightweight."

Fitz clicked on the same laptop to a second live video: A busy restaurant.

"Number eleven: the president pro tempore's at a late breakfast meeting."

He clicked to a third video: a ranch house.

"Number ten: the Secretary of State's a guest in Texas at the home of a billionaire buddy. Two for one."

Click to a stately two-story white mansion surrounded by trees.

"Number nine: the VP. He's at his residence in D.C. Scheduled to leave in an hour. He won't."

Fitz looked back at Franklin.

"These guys may go last. Meaning around five or so after ten. They may just be getting word of the attacks. But it won't matter."

Fitz scooted his chair to the second laptop.

A building on Wall Street.

"Number eight: the Treasury Secretary. Having a 9:30 meeting with the Big Banks' Big Three. They actually share Number two with two other guys, because of their power over Congress and influence over Caesar. So this meeting hit is a Big Four-in-one."

He looked back at Franklin again.

"That's it for the Presidential Succession Gang. You probably thought we'd stop there, didn't you?"

Smirk. Then back to the second laptop. 9:48 am.

Click. A building complex. Slow zoom to an office window. A young man at a desk, on the phone.

"Number seven: the Social Media Billionaire Guy. At his desk early in California. Last day."

Click to a private jet on a runway, waiting for takeoff.

"Number six: The Online Book-Sales Billionaire. Last flight."

Click to a high, long video shot looking down on a packed auditorium, now zooming in on three men seated by the on-stage podium, then on the oldest of the three.

"Number five: The Insurance Billionaire Guy. Last policy."

Fitz laughed softly at that. Scooted his chair to the third laptop, complaining, "Damn, I shoulda got an office chair with rollers."

Franklin, limp and aware, started silently, weakly to pray, repeating the single word over and over: "Help …"

Click. A yacht on the ocean. A slow zoom.

"Number four: The News Media Billionaire Guy. Last report."

Click. A limo rolling on a highway.

"Number three: The Computer Billionaire Guy. Last byte."

Click. A mansion in a wooded area.

"Number two: The Billionaire Brothers who share this ranking with the Wall Street cronies. These two guys with tentacles from D.C. to each state legislature. The two families meeting for older brother's birthday. Last candle."

Click. Alternating videos of a New York high-rise.

"Number one: Caesar at his Manhattan pad, meeting at 10:00 am with the Big Russian Bear … who I see … in this one scene … is walking in the front door as I speak. The early bird …."

Fitz checked the laptop's three digital clocks: 9:52.

He moved back to the first laptop.

Click. "I need immediate voice check and reports on location of targets. Number twelve?"

A disguised voice, sounding like a bass 45 rpm recording on 33⅓. As Fitz checked with each of the twelve numbers, the voice was disguised, most bass, a couple high, one like a child, one a dwarf in a Disney film. All okayed visual views of targets.

"Okay," Fitz said calmly, turning back and checking on Franklin.

"I wish you'd have gone with us," he told him. Franklin only stared at him, then glanced at each laptop as Fitz continued, "You're about to see a blazing variety: Drones. Many missiles. Sharpshooters. All hidden and appearing so fast, there's no defense.

"Oh. You wondering how I could get money to fund such an arsenal? Not all billionaires are oligarchs. A couple still actually believe in the Constitution." He looked closer at Franklin's eyes, then smiled and winked. "And not all billionaires are American. The biggies have their own selective networks, don't they?"

The phone in Franklin's pocket buzzed softly. Fitz looked there. Then at Franklin.

"Guess you're loved and being checked on. That's nice."

Fitz sat at the first laptop, leaning back, waiting, watching the clock digits change. He turned back and gazed at Franklin.

"Time in the movies when the cavalry rides in and saves the day, right buddy? Not today."

Then: 10:00.

Fitz quickly reached over to each laptop, flipping a button and calling out, “Okay! All systems go! Report in as I call your Number! I’m checking the videos as I can!”

One by one, Fitz checked all twelve videos. One by one, within seven minutes, the disguised voices all reported, “AOK.”

Then silence.

Fitz sat still, then clicked again, reviewing all twelve videos. Silent blazes flared in most. The other live videos also mute: One plane exploded. One flaming and crashing. The sinking yacht’s bow disappearing into the deep. The New York office building hit by missiles from all four sides, the top half melting and falling to Fifth Avenue and its side streets. All in silence.

Franklin, of course, recalled 9/11. His eyes were filling up, making it difficult to see.

Fitz leaned back. Thought a long moment. Then he closed each laptop. Unplugged and put them in a roomy carry bag, zipped it up.

He reached in his jacket and pulled out a small trash bag and a small plastic bottle with a spray cap. He grabbed the two teacups, sprayed and wiped them down with a handkerchief, placing the cups in the trash bag.

Then he rose, walking out of the room, the sound of his feet descending the old wooden stairs. In a few moments, he returned wearing rubber gloves, wiping down the table with a towel, and placing a large water bottle on it, then wiping the bottle down. He sprayed and wiped the chairs top to bottom, then anything else around the room.

Fitz got down on his haunches and stared at Franklin.

"Okay, buddy. We got the fascists. We got the oligarchs. Hopefully, the general can restore order after a few days of chaos. Maybe he can move it back closer to a democracy. Maybe not. We'll see how it goes. We may have to go to a phase two."

Fitz checked Franklin's breathing, his pulse, his eyes. He pulled out a clean handkerchief and wiped them clear of tears.

"Here's the deal," Fitz said. "You may go to sleep. You may not. You should get your faculties back in another four to six hours. Your respirator's good for twenty-four, so you should be fine. You'll be dehydrated when you come out from under, so you've got water there. Be sure and drink it so your head will be clearer. Maybe not totally clear, but clearer. You'll need that to remember what I tell you now:

"I've wiped down the entire place. I've bagged everything I can and will toss it. I've been incognito here. I don't expect any feds or cops to know about this place. If they somehow find out, it probably won't be for at least a day or two.

"But you need to vamoose as soon as you can. You don't want to be connected to this at all … and I don't want you to be. I'm putting an extra-large trash bag right here. When you're able to move, roll up the cot mattress and pillow. The respirator. Stuff them in the bag. Take it out with you. There's a dumpster on the street corner a block away. North. Toss it in there. They regularly pick it up in the late afternoon. If you think of anything you've touched that I haven't wiped down, wipe it down."

Fitz studied Franklin.

"I'm going underground now. You won't see me again. I'll lock the door, so no unexpected wanderer appears. Just leave it unlocked when you go. Wipe the door knobs down, so no prints."

He gave a final leg pat, grabbed his laptops satchel and the small trash bag, hurried through the room and down the steps.

Franklin barely heard the distant door close. He felt his eyes filling again. He was thinking of Evelyn, of Cassie. Among the chaos of news reports, they'd hear about the American and Russian presidents in New York. They'd think of Franklin here, be worried sick.

He lay there and prayed. And prayed. Exhausted, he began to drift off.

He didn't know how long it took to come to. His eyes slowly opened. Light from the windows was fading. He tried to move his arms, his legs. They slowly, reluctantly responded. Finally, he was able to sit up. His head ached terribly, as if two powerful, pressing hands were attempting to crush his skull. He removed the tubes from his nose, tested his breathing. It seemed fine.

He rocked, rose slowly to his feet. Got the water bottle and sat back down. Opened and slowly drank until he had consumed half of it.

Then he rose again, rolled the cot and pillow up, took the respirator, stuffed them in the trash bag. Stuck the water bottle in his backpack. Grabbed and donned his jacket and cap, and mounted the backpack on his shoulders. Pulled a handkerchief from his back pocket and wiped down the bed frame. In this day of DNA, he knew he couldn't wipe it clean enough.

Time to go.

He carried the trash bag out with him. Moved cautiously out of the yard, through the gate and on to the street. It was nearly deserted, except for a couple of people wandering aimlessly, in shock from the day's events. Sirens continued to wail in the distance. Smoke and the death stench still rose from Midtown, where the attack had occurred.

A block from the townhouse, Franklin found the dumpster. He deposited the trash bag, turned, and headed away. The city would basically be locked down, like during 9/11. He decided he would go back to the small hotel.

Entering the tight, pristine lobby, the lovely desk clerk stared sadly at him.

"My god," she gasped weakly. "Are you okay?"

Franklin nodded yes.

"What's happening to our nation?" she moaned desperately. "What's going to happen to us?"

“This is America. We’ll be fine,” Franklin lied. Then said honestly, “I need to call my daughter, my girl. They’ll be worried.”

“Sure,” the clerk muttered. “I’m glad you’re okay.”

“You too,” Franklin said, moving to the stairs.

Closing the hotel room’s door, he slipped out of the backpack, the jacket and cap, grabbed the water bottle and flopped exhausted on the bed. He took a long swig. Closed his eyes, asked for guidance. Then pulled out his phone.

He called Evelyn first. They cried together.

He called Cassie. They sat silently, saying little, just hearing each other breathe.

Finally, she sighed, gently offering, “I don’t know what story or book you had in mind when you went up there. But you’ve got one now, haven’t you?”

Franklin lay there, not answering.

“Reeves?”

“Yes,” he finally answered softly. “Yes, babe. I’ve got one now.”

READER RESOURCES

Q & A WITH AUTHOR ROGER ARMBRUST

Q Who is your novel, *Pressing Freedom*, for?

A *Pressing Freedom* is a novel for readers drawn to the entire human condition, ranging from the individual's deep involvement in family and romantic relationships, spiritual concepts, professional life, local and national political affairs, and even mysteries.

Novelist Webb Hubbell points out in his endorsement that it's a thriller within a thriller, so it's a double-stamp day for any fan of intrigue.

But it also draws readers heavily into the protagonist's past: his own secret, violent military history; his later battle with alcoholism, and effort to lead an honest life as journalist, poet, father, and lover. Readers naturally begin comparing their own personal conditions to those of a novel's characters.

So they should be prepared to take on the protagonist's specific experiences in these areas, and of other characters introduced as the novel's thriller-within-a-thriller unfolds.

This book is also for any reader concerned about the state of one's community, nation and their relationship with the world. Because events in Far River (the protagonist's small-city home) or in New York (where he spent two decades working) can impact humans in other locations as well, perhaps even nationally and internationally.

Q What's in store for the reader?

A The reader will grasp, through the protagonist's present experience, a dramatic view of a small city's personal relationships, politics, and undercurrent of crime. Also how a single act can lead an alert journalist to a greater mystery, and an effort to unravel its tangled strings.

Then how this local mystery forces him back to contacts from his violent past, relying on their protection, and suddenly discovering a separate, sinister plot unfolding which can impact the entire nation and the world. Should he get involved? If so, where should his loyalty lie? What should he do?

As the plots unfold, the reader should also glean a sense of press freedom: how a local (or statewide) newspaper operates; its mission to monitor, stalk, and even fight to find the truth, and make government and business accountable for their public responsibilities, and especially commission of crimes.

As the novel progresses, the reader will travel with the protagonist back to New York, walk its streets as he activates his journalistic and past assassin's sense in investigating and uncovering the specific effort to take down the nation's leadership, an attempt to both make and control history.

Perhaps most of all, readers will gain insight into a character's attempting to amend a secret, violent past, and replacing it with a spiritual base that will support his effort to lead an honest, caring, impactful personal and professional life. They'll also see the vital importance of memory on measuring where he stands in the universe; on how a haunting past can weigh on present decisions and actions; and how former love relationships never really leave, but hover in the corner, waiting to force their way back into the evening's dramatic dance.

Readers should also glean new insight into why today's America is in trouble. The characters are sensitively aware of it, discuss it, unsure what to do about it. Then the protagonist discovers that someone is prepared to do something about it, and must decide if he should respond to that, and how. American and world readers will experience how the protagonist responds. They may question those responses. But they'll know it's their America and world he's bound to, and particularly America's Constitution. And they should rightly question how they would respond.

Q To what extent is the plot driven by actual events? Or by your prognostication of near-future events?

A On the fictional, local Far River scene, an event like the one described early in the novel actually occurred in my hometown back in the '70s, when I worked as a newspaper reporter. I was only aware of the specific original action—a shooting by police. What resulted from that, I don't know. I left the paper soon after, and lost contact with how any investigation might have progressed. But the event stayed with me for years, evidently intriguing the Muse, and keeping her whispering in my ear.

That memory stayed dormant until recently when events in Washington took their dramatic turn, moving our nation's former democracy from its position as a de facto oligarchy into a sudden lurch toward fascism.

Having been involved for decades in both journalism and poetry, in both writing and editing, I began to question how the nation would respond, how individuals would react if they considered the situation no longer tolerable. What sort of person or persons would react? And with what specific actions? And was there a way to somehow connect the local action in Far River with the greater peril being planned?

Q Why did you choose to tell parts of the story with inserted poems?

A Reeves Franklin, the protagonist—through trying to live an honest life while protecting a secret past—is a man guarded and calculating in his conversations, including with his lover Cassie. But his poetry allows him to express his spiritual, loving self, especially to her, to his daughter, and even to his higher power. It seems to work as therapy as well as an avenue of loving care.

Cassie, now a creative writer through her novels, doesn't question the poems he gives her. Doesn't ask what they "mean." She accepts them for what they are: artistic caresses within their loving continuum.

Q What got you started writing it? What kept you busy finishing it?

A The last four years, I had been writing columns on politics and economics for *The Clyde Fitch Report*, an arts/politics blog based in New York City. These included a column following the November 2014 national elections entitled "As U.S. Austerity Deepens, Prepare for Revolution," stating that, hopefully, the revolution would be peaceful, but it might not be. Then after the November 2016 national elections, I headlined a column "Prepare to Fight Fascism: 2017 and Beyond." I could foresee the nation, now turning from a de facto oligarchy into a fascist state, perhaps getting mired so deep that it couldn't crawl out.

The issue is so great, I could only envision a novel taking

on events that might dramatically alter the nation's political reality. I've always liked stories about one person, or a small group, stumbling into unplanned situations, finding themselves in an environment outside their control, being left with only forced decisions of faith and action in order to survive, maybe even prevail, but maybe not.

Q The novel form is a new venture for you, a longtime journalist and poet. Why did you take that step into the unknown?

A Parkhurst Brothers Publishers had already published my books of poetry. Ted Parkhurst had also encouraged me for years to write a book on my creative philosophy, which should be out in 2018. It's entitled *Go Deep. Take Chances*, with the subtitle *Embracing the Muse and Creative Writing.* In it, I encourage creative writers to trust the Muse and to dive in. That's basically what led me to take on this extended effort, moving from 1,000-word political columns and fourteen-line sonnets to a 40,000-word novel. I've no doubt it was the Muse more than me who connected the dots, blending both the Far River and New York mysteries, the protagonist's secret military life, and later intense personal relationships. And the faith and energy to move forward and complete the writing.

Q You are the father of an adult daughter who lives in another state. How has that dynamic informed your choice to give the protagonist a similar family connection? What about the protagonist's feelings was derived from your love for your daughter, and your concerns for her?

A Rainer Maria Rilke, in his *Letters to a Young Poet,* basically suggests if you MUST write, then integrate your experience, imagination, and dreams. That's what I've attempted to do in my creative writing, whether poetry, short story, screenplay, or novel.

This applies to *Pressing Freedom*, transferring my experience with an adult daughter to Reeves Franklin and his daughter Evelyn, but moving from fact to fiction: letting imagination and dream alter that relationship, and every relationship in the story, to create another reality.

This dance of reality, imagination, and dream forms the joy of the creative process. You think, "What if I felt my daughter was in danger? What would I do?" Then you measure that against the character of the protagonist: Would he do the same thing? With his imaginary personality and experience, would he do something else? And you trust the Muse to lead you through the dance.

AUTHOR BIOGRAPHY

Roger Armbrust, a native of Little Rock, Arkansas, was educated at Little Rock Catholic High School for Boys and the University of Arkansas at Little Rock (UALR). His journalism career began at the *Arkansas Democrat*, a statewide newspaper. Later, he taught creative and business writing at New York University while also serving as national news editor at *Backstage Magazine*, a position he held for ten years.

After returning to his native Little Rock, Armbrust edited the biography of former governor and United States Senator David Pryor. He continues to edit and publish both journalistically and creatively. His books of poetry *The Aesthetic Astronaut* and *oh, touch me there* were published by Parkhurst Brothers Publishers in 2010 and 2014, respectively.

Armbrust has one daughter, Catherine, who teaches in the Art Department of the University of Missouri.

A PREVIEW:
Go Deep. Take Chances. Embracing the Muse and Creative Writing

IN HIS NOVEL *PRESSING FREEDOM*, Roger Armbrust's protagonist Reeves Franklin will take time to write sonnets, asking the Muse for guidance before writing and thanking her after. It's a process Armbrust himself uses in creative writing, which he covers in his book, to be published by Parkhurst Brothers in 2018. Here is Armbrust's chapter introducing this process:

Go Deep

After one of my professional-writing classes at NYU, a student came up to me and asked, "Why do you write?"

I responded, "Do you mean poetry, which I consider the most important writing that I do?"

"Well, yes."

"Because it's the closest thing I know to a spiritual experience."

She seemed a bit stunned by that, so I decided to put

the statement in perspective.

"I didn't come up with that idea," I stated, smiling. "Homer opens *The Odyssey* by saying, 'Sing to me of the man, Muse…' He's calling on this higher power to communicate to him and through him, that he may tell a wonderful story."

Indeed, the classical creators all seemed to understand the need to go deep, to tap into that conscious contact with a powerful resource both within and outside them. The Greeks and Romans called on a Muse, one of the nine goddesses of poetry, song, the arts and sciences.

In the eighth or ninth century BC (depending on who you talk to) the Greek poet Homer, this time in *The Iliad*, opens with the prayer, "Rage—Goddess, sing the rage of Peleus' son Achilles…" Some 800 years later, the Roman poet Virgil entreats as he begins *The Aeneid*, "Tell me the reason, Muse…"

Now, move up to the wonderful Russian poet Anna Akhmatova early in the 20th century:

The Muse

When at night I await her coming,
It seems that life hangs by a strand.
What are honors, what is youth, what is freedom,
Compared to that dear guest with rustic pipe in hand.
And she enters. Drawing aside her shawl
She gazed attentively at me.
I said to her: "Was it you who dictated to Dante
The page of The Inferno?" She replied: "It was I."

~

With this poem, Akhmatova provides two powerful messages for anyone who wants to move toward creative artistry:

First, if you want to write, you connect with the Muse, the Ultimate Reality, the Great Spirit, the Higher Power, the Great Breather, the God of God, Light of Light, True God of True God, the Intelligent Essence, the Endless Energy… call it what you will. The artist's job is to link up with that great voice of the universe which seems to sing within us and around us.

Second, we pay attention to what great literature has gone before us. In the case of Akhmatova's persona in "The Muse," she has witnessed this overwhelming force enter her room, toss back her shawl, and consider whether the young poet is ready for her. Akhmatova's persona wisely and humbly asks her awaited guest's identity by questioning whether her voice guided the Italian poet Dante through his literary masterpiece. And the Muse, always dedicated to brevity, provides her three-word answer, which in some translations from Russian to English becomes tightened to a single breath: "Yes."

So, there we have it. To thrive in the creative process, we call on the Great Voice of the Universe to sing through us, and we also make conscious contact with that voice by reading the great literature which sang before our writers' generation came into being.

How do you make that personal conscious contact with The Muse? That's up to you. I can only tell you how I do it. And that's basically the way Homer did it. I pray and listen. Not the prayer of any religion, except my personal religion of poetry, which fits within my belief of the great loving intelligent energy that creates and makes up all—stars and planets, air and earth, flesh and mind, birth and death, fear and destruction, faith and love.

What do I pray for? Most of all, to be honest and open-minded. How else can I faithfully go deep? How else can I fearlessly take chances? How else can I risk finding out who I really am and what life really is? How else can I translate that into a literary experience for myself and any other reader?

When I look at myself in relation to history and the universe, the truth is, I'm not much. I don't know much, and I haven't experienced much. And yet, through this conscious contact, I begin to understand my place on earth, in history and the universe, and the unique essence within me and around me. That's where, it seems to me, creative reading and creative writing take us.

It's a deep place. And it can prove a fearful, frustrating trek if we try to go it alone. I've done that. I can tell you there's a marked contrast in, first, taking on the relentless creative drive by myself—feeling only I possessed these flaming emotions, dramatic longings of experience, fear of death and of rejection, and stalwart belief that my first draft was the true word laid before all—and, later, the focused creative conversation arising when I open to the Muse's caress.

My experience tells me that, when you let go to the Muse, you find it. Open-minded conscious contact leads you to great reading, intense observation and involvement in the world, honest (and therefore real) relationships, and a clear, loving, unshakeable voice in your writing.

William James says we reach this place through faith and action. By faith, he seems to mean an individual's personal relationship with the divine. That's basically how he described it in his book *The Varieties of Religious Experience*, based on his series of lectures which didn't deal so much with religions, but with individuals' personal spiritual encounters.

James, who was a medical doctor, psychologist, philosopher and teacher—and older brother of the novelist Henry James—believed in concrete spiritual experiences. That is: humans' spiritual experiences lead to psychic changes, which in turn lead to changes in the way they think, feel, speak, write and live.

The Columbia University professor Wayne Proudfoot places James' view of concrete spiritual experiences into five categories: "voices and visions, responses to prayer, changes of heart, deliverances from fear, and assurances of support."

I believe we experience all those when we're involved in the creative-writing process. And I know that process can clarify existence for us, and bring change to our lives, and even to others, whether we writers immediately realize it or not, and whether a reader expects it or not.

Nikola Tesla in 1870, at age twenty-four, reciting aloud from Johann Wolfgang von Goethe's verse drama *Faust*, suddenly foresaw AC currents propelling induction motors—technology which didn't exist. His great idea would lead to electric power grids, and stun thousands at Chicago's World's Fair when he presented a *City of Light*. His design eventually would shower the globe with energy and light, changing the way people worked and lived.

What were the specific lines that helped poetry shake science? Tesla, later called the Father of Physics, cited these:

> The glow retreats, done is the day of toil;
> It yonder hastes, new fields of life exploring;
> Ah, that no wing can lift me from the soil
> Upon its track to follow, follow soaring!

What does that tell you about the power of creative writing? The German Goethe, who died twenty-four years before Tesla's birth in the Balkans, probably didn't say to himself, "Well, I think I'll write *Faust*, and it will help Tesla scientifically change civilization." Knowing the creative process's power, including its psychic potential, he could have! And Goethe did perform research in the natural sciences. But the odds are, while expecting society's advancement, he probably didn't specifically foresee Tesla, or his own verse causing such a tremendous technological impact.

But can you see how the creative process not only ignites the writer's imagination, but the reader's? Writing's imagery and rhythms invite both creator and recipient to explore and expand their worlds, and can induce an endless flowering of understanding and growth. The creative connection between writer and Muse and reader can, if one considers Tesla's experience, literally change the individual, and perhaps even the world.

Still, I believe this only can occur when writers trust the Muse and their own experience, imagination, and dreams, and don't concern themselves with how a reader might react. One might worry about that in some other writing form, such as business or governmental reports, but not in creative writing. Here, our job is to not limit ourselves, or restrict ourselves with any reader's limits. We write to grow, and invite any reader to grow also.

"I have only three criteria for what I go on reading and teaching: aesthetic splendor, intellectual power, wisdom," says Yale scholar and writer Harold Bloom in his book *Where Shall Wisdom Be Found?* "Societal pressures and journalistic fashions may obscure these standards for a time, but mere Period Pieces never endure. The mind always returns to its needs for beauty, truth and insight. Mortality hovers, and all of us learn the triumph of time."

With that in mind, isn't it best to use our limited time

well? And what better way than going deep and taking chances through the creative process.

For more sonnets by the author and more novels from the publisher, point your browser to: www.parkhurstbrothers.com